THE LAWS OF MAGIC

By Greg Fowlkes

Includes the Special Bonus Story
HORRORSCOPE

And introducing THE FICTIONAL DETECTIVE,
A Fictional Press Novel.

THE LAWS OF MAGIC

© 2010 The Fictional Press
www.TheFictionalPress.com

Published by Intrepid Ink, LLC

Intrepid Ink, LLC provides full publishing services to authors of fiction and non-fiction books, eBooks and websites. From editing to formatting, to publishing, to marketing, Intrepid Ink gets your creative works into the hands of the people who want to read them.

Find out more at www.IntrepidInk.com.

ISBN 13: 978-1-935774-20-4

Printed in the United States of America

FOREWORD

I wrote the first two stories in this series "Wizard at Law" and "Night Battles" back in the 70's. I had started writing in graduate school churning out four novels and quite a few stories and novellas, but not actually getting anything published. I eventually graduated — in other words, they gave me a degree when I wasn't looking and kicked me out — and so I got a job writing software. It paid pretty well and it took away the financial incentive for trying to get things published. I continued to write for a while, but with four novels started and never finished, after a time I lost the need to write. This explains the lapse of nearly thirty years between "Night Battles" and the next story, "Do Vampires Not Bleed," which I wrote mostly to see if I could still do it. I was rather pleased with the results.

Technologies have change since I first started writing, and print on demand has made it feasible to avoid the necessity of interesting a publisher in your works. This led to the formation of The Fictional Press and my first published book, *The Fictional Detective*. It seemed like a good idea to issue a volume of the Egil Njalsson stories, and to round things out and explain the relationship between Egil and Jack I wrote "Without License".

The first two stories have endured a tortuous existence, the first having been written on a typewriter, transcribed to WordStar on a CP/M computer using 8" floppies to be joined by the second, thence to WordStar on a DOS PC using 3 1/4" and finally to Word Perfect on a Windows XP machine. It's amazing that they have survived at all.

They say that authors should write about what they know best. This poses certain problems when the subject is an alternate universe that exists only in the author's head. However, several facets of Njalsson's world impinge upon our own reality.

The university where Njalsson completed his undergraduate education, The California Institute of Thaumaturgy or CalThaum is loosely based on the California Institute of Technology where I made an all too brief beginning of my college life. CalThaum is no Hogwarts, but a thoroughly modern research university dedicated to the study of metaphysics. Unfortunately, Njalsson received his undergraduate degree during a recession, hence his excursion into law.

The story "Night Battles" was inspired by the book *The Night Battles: Witchcraft and Agrarian Cults in the Sixteenth and Seventeenth Centuries* by Carlo Ginzburg. In this book Ginzburg wrote about a cult of "benandanti" who believed that they battled with evil witches during dreams. I took as my premise that these battles were not only real, but that there were modern day members of the cult that still carried on the struggle.

The rest of the details of the various stories came from my imagination as colored by diverse and extensive readings on subjects such as ethnology, physics, history, archeology, and technology as well as liberal doses of popular culture. Authors that have influenced me have included Robert Heinlein (who first incorporated magic), Randall Garrett, and Glen Cook, as well as many others.

Finally, I would like to thank Irene Cash and Intrepid Ink Publishing, without whom this volume would never have been published.

Greg Fowlkes
Author
The Fictional Press
www.TheFictionalPress.com

TABLE OF CONTENTS

☆　☆　☆　☆　☆

WITHOUT LICENSE

WITHOUT LICENSE

☆　　☆　　☆　　☆　　☆

As Egil Njalsson climbed the steps of the criminal courts building he wondered if it was really worth it. Eighteen months of practicing law on his own and here he was in his only suit, about to attend the preliminary hearing in a petty case for which with luck he would be able to recover his expenses. It wasn't even a paying client. The state would be picking up the tab for this one, and he'd ended up being the lawyer appointed by the court. At the moment it wasn't clear who would benefit most from the charity, the client or the lawyer. He hadn't had a case in three months and he'd just been eking out a living writing briefs for other lawyers. He could do that well enough. His technical background gave him a depth of knowledge most lawyers lacked when it came to cases involving points of science as well as law. If he hadn't had that he'd be starving.

He'd been thinking about that a lot lately; whether he had made the right decision giving up science and going into the law. At the time, with the aerospace industry in a depression in the early seventies, it had seemed like a good idea. Engineers were pumping gas and PhD's in physics were selling insurance. Being a lawyer had seemed like a good way to make money. A stable income, no ups and downs. He'd put in his time at law school and done well. After the grind at CalThaum, law school had been a snap. So here he was a lawyer barely making ends meet and his school mates, the ones who had stuck with science were all making it rich designing personal calculating engines and disk storage units.

He tried to put all these thoughts out of his mind as he passed through the big brass doors of the court house. After all, he did have a client to defend, and a duty to him. It wasn't easy, though. It wasn't, after all, a very important case. Just a charge of fortune telling and practicing the Art without a license. Minor offenses, probably not even any jail time involved. This wouldn't even be a trial today, just a plea and arranging of bail.

It wouldn't even have amounted to that if his client hadn't instisted on pleading not guilty. He'd met him at the county jail, an old man, one Jake Schmidts. He'd tried to talk him out of pleading not guilty, too. A guilty plea, a small fine, and they both could be done with it. His client, though, had turned out to be something of a character. So here he was.

It took an hour and a half before their case came up. The judge looked at him questioningly when he had pleaded not guilty, but thankfully had released his client on his own recognizance when he indicated he had a permanent address. It was over in five minutes.

They got the release papers and the court date from the bailiff. Egil started to head out when he noticed that his client seemed lost and disoriented by it all. "Do you have car fare home?"

"No," Schmidts said. "I didn't have any money on me when they came and arrested me. Not a cent."

"Which way do you live?"

The old man gave an address on Fair Oaks Street. It wasn't far out of his way. Neither one of them lived in the best part of town.

"I can give you a lift," Egil said.

"That's kind of you, Mr. Njalsson," Schmidts said. The mister was ironic. The arrest report hadn't given an age, just 'somewhere around seventy." As far as Egil could tell that might have been off by a decade or two.

The address turned out to be a sort of second hand junk store. The operative word was junk. If the pieces in the dirty window were the best of the lot then Egil could see how Schmidts qualified as indigent.

"Thanks for the ride. I've a beer inside if you'd like."

Njalsson looked at his watch. It wasn't too early to start drinking, at least just a beer. The work at the office would wait. He had to talk to Schmidts anyway to prepare a case. Besides, the old man seemed to want to pay him back for the ride.

If anything, the shop was worse on the inside than it looked from the front. Odd bits of bric-a-brac were strewn around everywhere; most of it looking like it hadn't been moved or even dusted in twenty years. Broken down pieces of furniture were covered with moldering sheets.

The old man led him to the back and up some stairs to an apartment above the shop. The kitchen was cleaner, though still hardly spotless. Of course, Egil's own small apartment wasn't the neatest of place, either.

The refrigerator looked as old as Schmidt's, but the beer was cold. Schmidt's took out two and motioned him to a chair at the kitchen table.

"So what happens now, Mr. Njalsson?"

"The trial will be held on the date on the summons. The district attorney will call his witnesses and make his case. Then I'll make my case. The judge will then decide."

"No jury?" Schmidt's asked disappointedly.

"Not unless we've got a very strong case to present. This is a small matter. It's better left to a judge. A jury would be considered a waste of time, I'm afraid, and would probably result in a higher fine. Maybe even jail."

"So you think I'm guilty?"

"I don't think you have much of a case."

"That's different?"

"To a lawyer it is."

Schmidts snorted in disgust.

"I don't want to disillusion you, Mr. Schmidts, but you've got to face the facts. Do you have a license to practice Magic?"

"No."

"Did you tell the fortune of one Mrs. Einar Johnson?"

"Yes, and an ungrateful woman she is, too. Just because I told her the truth about that shifty salesman she thinks is going to marry her. He's just after her late husband's money."

Egil raised an eyebrow.

"It's the truth. I've been reading the cards longer than you've been alive, Mr. Njalsson, and I know what I'm doing. That salesman is the one that got her to swear out a complaint against me."

"It doesn't matter whether what you said was the truth or not. What matters is that you were practicing the Art without a license. Magic is a potentially dangerous business. It's not something that untrained people should be dealing with. That's what the law is about."

"What would you know about the Art, Mr. Lawyer?" Schmidts asked sharply.

"I know more than most, Mr. Schmidts. I studied applied metaphysics at the California Institute of Thaumaturgy for four years before going into the law. I've got a Bachelor's of Science degree. I've also got my practitioner's license from both the state of California and Wisconsin. I may not be the greatest practitioner of the Art, but I am competent enough to know what I am and am not capable of."

"So maybe you did study at a fancy school out west. Those scientists don't know everything. They think that they've discovered magic, but magic goes back. Way back. Back before Helmholtz and Gauss. Before the Egyptians and Babylonians. Magic is old, Mr. Njalsson, and the doctors and professors haven't learned half of it."

"And you have?" Egil asked sarcastically. He was getting annoyed at the old man's pretensions of knowledge. He was surprised, though, that Schmidts knew that the two physicists Helmholtz and Gauss had been instrumental in proving the scientific basis for magic.

"No. I'm no fool. I've been studying the Art all my life. I know what I know and I have a good idea of what I don't. What I do know is more than a youngster like you learns in four years at college, even if it is a fancy one."

"Look, Mr. Schmidts," Egil said. "This isn't working out. Maybe you should get yourself a different lawyer."

The old man looked at him in surprise, then shook his head. "No. I guess you were just telling me the way it is. I may not like it, but I can't fault you for telling the truth."

"Okay. Is there anything I can use in your defense?"

"Guess not."

"Well, where did you learn to tell fortunes, to read the cards?" Egil asked.

"From an old Romany woman," the old man answered.

"Where? Here in the city?"

"No, it was a long time ago. Bohemia, I think it was."

"Bohemia? You mean Czechoslovakia."

"Yes, that's what they call it now I think. Prague. I was a student there."

"A student? At a university? I thought you didn't believe in learning."

"I was younger then. I thought there were things I might learn. I was wrong."

"Did you get a degree, though? That might carry some weight, especially a foreign one."

"Wait a moment. I think I have one someplace. Let me go look." Schmidts went down to his shop. From below Egil could hear noises as if boxes were being moved around. He didn't quite know what to make of the old man's gypsy tale. Bohemia had become part of Czechoslovakia after the First World War in the breakup of the Austrian Empire. It hadn't been a separate country since the Hapsburgs.

There were footsteps on the stairway and Schmidts showed up with a small picture frame carrying a piece of parchment. It was certainly a degree, but not from the University of Prague. The writing had faded with age and Egil had never learned French, but it appeared to be a doctorate granted by the Sorbonne. It was also made out to one Jacques Krieger.

"This isn't your name."

"It was the name I was using then."

"Can you prove that?"

"Not that I can see."

"Oh well. Maybe we can use it. If you can find anymore old papers like this save them for me. We might have some defense if we can prove you had an education, particularly if it was before the current examination system went into effect."

"I'll do that, Mr. Njalsson."

"Well I've got to get going now. Can I take this with me?" the lawyer asked, holding up the sheepskin.

"Yes, if it will help."

Egil let himself out through the shop. He dumped the diploma on the car seat next to him and started the car. While the engine was warming up he glanced down at it.

The date was written in Roman numerals. It took him a moment to figure out the year. It was 1847. Either the old man was lying to him or he might find himself defending him in a commitment hearing.

☆   ☆   ☆   ☆   ☆

The weeks before the trial passed without much in the way of a defense arising. His client changed his story several times, produced several pieces of evidence, none of which would hold up in court, and Egil kept trying to convince him to plead guilty, to no effect.

His own practice went on much as before; which is to say, without clients. However, he did receive a commission from a patent attorney to write a brief on the relevant prior art for a new process involving the Art. While patent law was not his strong point, the years at CalThaum had not been wasted. His knowledge of the scientific aspects of the Art went far beyond that of the average lawyer and at least a few attorneys were starting to use him to ghost briefs. In this case they were paying quite well.

He was returning to his office one night after stepping out for dinner at the corner coffee shop. The stairway of his building was dark, which wasn't surprising. His landlord had a habit of buying glow tubes with a second rate spell on them. They didn't last, but they were cheap. He stumbled as he reached the landing, pausing a moment to catch his balance.

Something alerted him then. A sixth sense, some smell or small noise. He wasn't sure. His paranormal abilities were slight, they'd been tested thoroughly in college, but his normal senses had been trained to compensate. It had been some time since they'd been exercised fully, but one thing the lab work had taught him was to put his trust in them.   He edged his way silently towards his office. Through the frosted glass of the door he could see the beam of a flashlight wavering around inside. He wasn't sure what to do. He was unarmed and unprepared, but he was also more than a little angry. There was a trick that he'd been good at, a simple magic of no great substance. It was all he had.

Putting his left hand on the doorknob he turned it slowly.   The noise inside continued.   When the latch released he braced himself, then popped the door open with his right hand extended palm outward. A brilliant ball of light flared from his hand then shot across the room. There was a shriek followed by the sound of a dropping flashlight. Though his own eyes had been shut, his vision still suffered somewhat from the afterimage of his Kirillian projection. He caught glimpses of a dark swirling shape of black leather like wings as the intruder shrank to the size of a bat and made for the open window. Egil was too stunned to do anything. It was just as well. He was unprepared to deal with a vampire.

He crossed over to the window, shutting and latching it firmly. He'd left it open while he went to dinner. The office lacked an air conditioning elemental. The landlord was too cheap to provide ariels to cool the offices. Only the building code forced him to provide a salamander in the basement for heat during the winter.

When Egil turned on the light he saw the mess that the intruder had made. One thing was certain, it wasn't a random burglary. The vampire had been after papers. Half the contents of his filing cabinets were on the floor, the folders opened and the papers strewn on the floor. The cashbox he kept in his desk had been opened, but the contents had been undisturbed; all twenty three dollars and eighty-two cents.

That left one other thing to worry about. Njalsson shut the door. He didn't want to be disturbed. He stepped up to where his degree hung on the outside wall of the office and removed the frame from its hook. He grabbed a piece of chalk from the desk drawer and drew a small pentagram on the wall closing the outer circle with a flourish. Inside he drew a nine pointed star consisting of three interlocking triangles. At each of the vertices he inscribed a name in Norse runes. In the center he wrote one last name then knocked on the figure with a ring inscribed with the complement of the pentagram.

The pentagram dissolved revealing a dark recess. It went back much farther than the width of the wall would seem to allow, but then the interior of his wall safe wasn't in the world of light. It was his own handiwork. Any commercial model he could have afforded wouldn't have stopped even an amateur. His spell of protection wasn't that powerful, but because it wasn't a commercial incantation a thief wouldn't be familiar with it. Not too many safecrackers were conversant in Norse, either. More than once Egil had been thankful that his Scandinavian heritage had led him to learning Norse as well as the more common Hebrew, Latin, and Greek used in the Art.

He reached into the safe, and reassured himself that the contents were untouched. His client had impressed upon him the need to keep the documents he was using absolutely secure. He was beginning to understand why. For the sake of thoroughness he checked to make sure that the diploma and dowser's license Jake had given him were safe as well.

He returned the documents to the safe. Standing back from the wall he uttered the locking word as he clapped his hands. The blank wall reappeared leaving only a faint dusting of chalk to slip down the plaster. He replaced his diploma and began the work of restoring his files. It was certain that he wouldn't be getting any more work done that night.

Schmidts' trial came up the next day. He met his client at the courthouse. They had to sit through two speeding tickets and a drunk and disorderly charge before his case came up. The prosecution made its case. The arresting officer read his report on the stand. The woman who had brought the charges testified. Egil cross-examined both of them. It wasn't much use. Schmidt's had told her fortune on several occasions. There was also a crystal ball, a tarot deck, and several other pieces of apparatus that had been taken as evidence.

His own presentation was nearly as brief. He refused to allow his client to take the stand. With the different stories he'd gotten from him he could imagine what the eager beaver from the D.A.'s office would do to him during cross-examination. He did present as evidence the dowser's license that had been granted to one Johan Schmidt in 1907 by the State of Pennsylvania. He had pleaded that his client was an old man unfamiliar with the law and not aware that he wasn't entitled to practice the Art in this state.

With a bored look on his face the judge had examined the license then summoned the prosecutor and Egil to the bench.

"I don't know if this license is valid or not. It certainly doesn't entitle your client to tell fortunes in this state. However, I see no indication of fraud or malice. Frankly, I think the complainant filed charges because she didn't like the sound of the truth. I'm willing to let the defendant off with a fine of ninety dollars and a suspended sentence and a strong admonition against practicing the Art without first obtaining a license from the State Board of Sorcery. Is that agreeable to both parties? If so we can stop wasting the court's time."

The prosecutor grumbled a bit but backed down when he saw the look on the judge's face. We stepped back from the bench and the judge banged his gavel.

"I find the defendant guilty as charged of one count of practicing the Art without a license and sentence him to ninety days and a fine of ninety dollars. The jail time is suspended on the condition that the defendant refrains from practicing the Art. Next case."

It was a lot better result than Egil had expected. The judge had been sympathetic. For him it was almost as good as a win. Schmidts took it differently. Egil explained the situation to him. He shrugged his shoulders. It turned out Schmidts didn't have the ninety dollars. The thought of Schmidts going to jail offended Egil's professional sense. He ended up paying the fine out of his own money with the understanding that it was a loan.

"Well, thanks, Mr. Njalsson. You did your best," Schmidts said.

"Sorry I couldn't get you off, but we didn't have much of a case," Egil said distractedly. The break in at his office was still bothering him. "Do you have car fare home?"

"Don't worry about it," Schmidts said. "I don't mean to butt in, Mr. Njalsson, but you seem troubled. Is something wrong?"

"No, it's just that someone broke into my office last night. They made a mess of the place."

"Did they get away with much?"

"Not that I can tell. Not money at least. But I have a lot of important papers. Client's files. Confidential stuff, you know. Whoever it was made such a mess of the place that I'm not sure what they got away with."

"That's too bad," Schmidts said, enough feeling in his voice for Egil to think he meant it. "Say, if you're going back there now I wouldn't mind a ride. It would save me waiting for a bus."

Egil shrugged, "Yeah, sure." It seemed out of character for his client. The old man had seemed proud, not willing to take charity from anyone without feeling an obligation. Still, the old man didn't have much of an income and eighty cents was a lot of money to him. He'd be able to walk to his place from the office.

Egil offered to drop him off on his way back to the office, but Schmidts had protested that he didn't want to take him out of his way. The lawyer hadn't wanted to push it. He figured that begging for a ride had cost the old man enough of his pride.

He parked his car in the lot behind the building and went up to the office. There was still a lot to straighten up. His filing system had never been that great, but the burglar had made total chaos of it. He was clutching a sheaf of papers in one hand just staring at the mess in confusion and anger when he noticed that Schmidts was standing in the doorway.

"I thought you were going home," Egil said in annoyance. He'd never figured the old man as the kind who got vicarious pleasure from other people's misfortunes.

"I thought you might need some help, Mr. Njalsson," Schmidts said apologetically. "Sure made a mess of things. Be glad to give you a hand."

Egil shrugged, his anger melting away. "I guess I could use the help at that. If you could just pick up the papers and put them in stacks, I can sort through them later. And you can stop calling me Mr. Njalsson. The name's Egil."

They spent the better part of the next two hours stacking and sorting papers. To the lawyer's surprise the old man seemed to have an uncanny knack of figuring out which papers went together. In fact he was doing better at restoring things than Egil himself was doing. By the time they were done most of the files were at least together if not properly alphabetized and the floor had been swept up.

"Thanks for the help. Would you care for a snort before you go?" Egil said pulling the pint bottle out of his desk drawer.

"Don't mind if I do, Egil," the old man said. The lawyer poured two healthy shots into a pair of water glasses that he kept in the drawer next to the bottle. He watched as the old man drank. He sipped the cheap whiskey slowly, not downing it in one gulp like a drunk.

"Well, I've got to get going. If I could just have my diploma and things from your safe I'll be on my way."

Egil started to remove the frame from the wall, then turned and asked, "How'd you know about the safe."

"I saw the spell marks on the wall. Good work, too. Don't see runes used much these days, all that fancy Greek and Hebrew," Schmidts commented professionally.

Egil eyed Schmidts critically. A first class wizard with a Ph.D. might be able to spot his spell, but it didn't figure that a second rate unlicensed fortune teller would be able to sense it, let alone tell what language the pentagram had been inscribed in. If Schmidts were that good he wouldn't have had any trouble getting a license.

"Do you mind telling me how you spotted it?"

"It's not so much what's there, as what's missing. Like I said, it's good work. But the wall was too blank. Made me curious. And of course my things were inside. I've had them a long time. The ties of sympathy are strong. I ken the runes, too, though I haven't used them in quite a space. They're not what I was brought up with."

"Well I'll be," Egil said shaking his head. "Guess there's no point in trying to conceal my spell. You've probably guessed it."

"I wouldn't do that, Egil. You've been good to me," Schmidts said stiffly.

"Yeah, okay." The lawyer went through the opening spell. The diploma and certificate were under the packet of patent information that he'd been working on. As he lifted up the envelope the old man straightened.

"That's what he was after. Those papers in the envelope."

"Who?" Egil asked suspiciously.

"The burglar. He was trying to steal those papers. The rest was just to conceal his actions."

"Do you know what these papers are?"

"No. Like I said, I don't pry where I don't have no business."

"What else do you know about the burglar?"

"Only what I sense. The aura. He was in a hurry. Afraid of being spotted. I can pick up the traces that he left."

Egil looked at the old man. There were such things as natural sensitives, people who could pick up the emotional wake left under certain circumstances. The police made use of them at times, but the talent was too rare and erratic to be commonplace.

"Any idea who he is or who he's working for?"

"No, but I might be able to find out."

"How?"

"Like I said, he left his traces. There are things that can be done to bring these out. Like the police lifting fingerprints. I can do it for you if you want."

"Be my guest," Egil said, half motivated by curiosity as to what Schmidts would do. As far as he knew, this kind of thing was beyond the current state of the Art.

The old man reached for the envelope. Egil let it slide from his hands. Placing the envelope on the desk, Schmidts poured out two fingers of the whiskey into his glass. The lawyer wondered if it were all a ploy to get another drink. He was asked to turn out the room lights, which left just the desk lamp to cast its glow in a sharp circle around the envelope. With a swift and sure movement the old man dipped the first and second finger of his left hand into the whiskey and traced a complicated figure in alcohol on top of the paper.

For a moment, nothing seemed to happen, but then as the whiskey began to evaporate in the heat from the lamp Schmidts stuck his nose over the paper and sniffed hard as if to draw all the vapor into his nose. His eyes were shut and all his concentration was on the scent. After a minute of this he stood and then began to walk around the room sniffing intently. At random he would open a filing cabinet drawer or poke his nose into a corner. He did this for fifteen minutes before sitting down and draining the remaining whiskey in his glass.

"What was that all about?" Egil asked.

"The Law of Sympathy. The thief was after these papers; therefore he was in a way bound to them. I in turn created a bond between the papers and myself by breathing in their essence. By the Transitive Principle this created a bond between the thief and myself. I then walked around the room sniffing his spoor trying to read his thoughts. He was agitated, in a hurry, so his scent was strong and lingering."

"It can't be done. You can tell what a man is thinking by smelling his sweat?"

"Why not? Your scientists talk about pheromones and such controlling animal behavior. A man is nothing more than a two legged animal. Never forget the nose. It is the oldest and surest sense, the one most difficult to fool. Too much is made today of learned languages and complicated rituals. More reliance should be placed on what is primal. The trained nose may reveal far more than the eye can perceive."

"What did your nose perceive, then?"

"Less than I had hoped for. Mostly the thief was thinking about where the papers might be and when you were coming back. He didn't think about his own identity at all, but then most people don't. I did get two things from him, though. One was the thought of ten thousand dollars. That was what he would get for turning over the papers. The other was a number. A telephone number that he was supposed to call when he had the papers in his possession."

Egil wrote down the number. "Is that it?"

"Yes, that's the number. Sorry that's all I could come up with," the old man said apologetically.

"Don't worry about it. That's a lot more than I expected."

"Look," Egil said, "It's obvious you know a lot more about the Art than you would need to get a license. Why don't you just apply for one?"

"You have to take a test. I'd never be able to pass. Most of the answers are wrong. If I knowingly gave the wrong answer just to pass the test, I'd be lying. The Art disapproves of falsehoods. I might lose my abilities. It took me a long time to earn those Powers."

"Well, if you ever change your mind, let me know. I'd be glad to help you out."

"Thank you. You're a good man. If you ever need help, you know where I live," Schmidts said. "Well, it's getting late so I'll be going now."

☆　☆　☆　☆　☆

After the old man had left, Egil called the patent attorney he'd been writing the brief for. If someone was trying to get the papers, his client should be informed. When Egil explained the situation to him, he was alarmed, but he didn't seem surprised.

"Do you mind my asking just what is so important about those papers? They looked like a routine application for a patent for an industrial process and the supporting documentation. If anything, there seems to be enough prior art to invalidate any patent application."

"That's kind of the point. I guess if someone broke into your office, this is no longer a secret. Our client — and I stress that so you understand that client attorney privilege applies to you — our client uses a process in their business that they currently pay royalties on. The royalties amount to twenty million dollars or so a year. They have discovered evidence of prior art that would invalidate that patent. That evidence is part of the supporting document. I wanted an independent opinion to make sure they are right. That's where you come in."

"I can see where twenty million a year would be a powerful motive for some people. Do you think the holders of the current patent might engage in some illegal activity?" Egil asked.

"The rights are owned by an intellectual property company called 'Consolidated Holdings'. They've been accused of some shady dealings in the past, but nothing's ever been proved. It's a privately held company, so it's hard to get information about them, but it's all kind of shadowy. A man named de Castro seems to be at the center of things, but it's impossible to find anything about him. It's almost like he doesn't exist."

"Thanks for the information," Egil said. "I should have the brief for you in a couple of days."

"Good. Oh, and Njalsson, be careful. From what I've heard, these guys play hardball. Several challenges to patents they hold have mysteriously been withdrawn before they've gone to court. In at least one case, the challenger just disappeared." With that he hung up.

Egil had a feeling that he was getting in over his head. He'd taken a job to write an opinion and now he found himself caught in the middle of a web of corporate espionage. He certainly wasn't getting paid to take those kinds of risks. But he didn't like the idea of someone coming in and trying to rob him. The question was, what was he going to do about it?

The paper with the telephone number Schmidts had come up with was staring him in the face. He could call it and see where it lead. That was a dumb idea. Right now whoever was behind this didn't know that he knew about them. If he called the number, they would know he knew, and that would put him at risk. On the other hand, if they were determined to get the papers he might be at risk already.

He'd call the number, but not from his office. They might have a spell on the other end to trace any callers. He'd have to take some precautions, and maybe work up a trace spell of his own. He pulled out his black bag from the bottom drawer of his filing cabinet and checked to make sure he had what he needed.

The first step was to find another phone that he could use. It would have to be a public phone, not too close to his office. He knew of a pay phone about ten blocks away. There wouldn't be much traffic around it this time of night that was important. He got his gear together and drove over to the phone.

He was in luck. The phone wasn't in use, and more importantly, it was working — never a sure thing in that neighborhood. He took a piece of chalk from his bag and began to draw a pentagram around the booth. He had a hunch that he might need some protection. He stepped inside the pentagram and sealed it with a final flourish.

After closing the door he lifted the handset off of its cradle and wrapped a black ribbon around the cord, tying it with a complicated knot meant to confuse any demons that might be sent down the wire. He took out a shallow glass bowl and filled it with mercury. He wound the phone cord so that it encircled the bowl. He placed a compass next to the bowl. The small shelf under the phone was getting crowded. Finally, he took his handkerchief and placed it over the mouth piece. This last move had no magical significance but would disguise his voice. He took a quarter from his pocket, dropped it in the slot, and dialed the number.

The phone rang three times before it was answered.

"I told you not to call this number," a gruff voice answered. At the same time, a face appeared in the bowl of mercury. The background appeared to be an office, but it was hard to tell in the small bowl. A look of suspicion crossed the face in the mercury. Egil noted the direction the compass pointed to and made a quick sketch of the face to help is memory.

"I'm sorry; I must have the wrong number. Who is this?" Egil asked. He didn't expect an answer, but he might get lucky.

"Who is this?" the voice demanded. "You don't know who you're messing with."

Egil hung up the phone quickly. He had a feeling he had gotten as much information as he was going to, and he didn't want to linger around any longer than he had to. He packed up his gear and removed the ribbon from the phone. He was smudging the pentagram outside when a police car stopped.

"Just what do you think you're up to there?" the cop asked, leaning out the window of the squad.

"Nothing, Officer. I was just making a phone call."

"And what would those chalk marks be. You wouldn't be trying to defraud the phone company now, would you?"

The cop got out of the car. He was beefy in a muscular way and a couple inches taller than Egil. "Let's see some ID."

Egil was fishing for his wallet when as flash of light and a puff of smoke appeared in the phone booth. When the smoke cleared there was nothing left inside but a charred puddle of plastic.

"Jesus, Mary Mother of God," the cop swore. "You sure seemed to have gotten someone's attention. Do you mind telling me what this is about?"

"It's late, officer," Egil explained. "I guess I must have woken him. He can be kind of cranky when he doesn't get enough sleep."

"Yeah, and I'm the pope's brother. You'd better give me some straight answers or I'll run you in for destroying private property."

Egil tried to explain giving just enough details to keep the cop happy, but without telling too much. The cop seemed to buy his story, or at least most of it.

As an afterthought, Egil showed the cop the picture he had sketched.

"You're not much of an artist, councilor, but that looks a lot like Tony de Castro. You'd better hope he wasn't the guy on the other end of the line. He's bad news."

"Thanks for the warning, officer," Egil said. "I'll watch out."

"You do that. And if you got anything on him that'll stick in a court, let me know. The department would love to send him away. They might even make me a sergeant. The name is O'Neil, Joseph O'Neil."

The cop gave him a card with his number on it, then got back in his car. There didn't seem to be any point in sticking around, so Egil did the same and drove back to his office.

☆   ☆   ☆   ☆   ☆

Egil was scared. This was something outside his experience. Someone had tried to kill him using the Black Arts. That was something he hadn't been taught at CalThaum. The dark side of magic wasn't taught anywhere. Black magic, as opposed to white or green magic, was proscribed by law, and no university in the world taught its practice or even its principals. A few graduate level courses might delve into defenses against the black arts, but he had only taken one such course and that had been years ago. There was only one person who might have the knowledge to defend him, and that was Jake Schmidts.

He drove past Jake's shop and when he saw that the light was still on in the second floor window he stopped. It took a few minutes, but Jack eventually came to the door. The shade was pulled back, and when he saw who it was, he opened the door.

"Something has happened, hasn't it?" Schmidts asked.

"Yes. Someone tried to kill me," Egil answered.

"How?"

"In a phone booth. The phone exploded. If I had still been in the booth, I'd be dead."

"Quick, take me to this booth. I need to see it before anyone touches it," Jake ordered.

They got in Egil's car and drove back to the pay phone. Jake got out and examined the booth and its surroundings, sniffing the air like a bloodhound. He got down on his knees to look closer at where Egil had erased the chalk lines.

"Did the phone explode before or after you erased the pentagram?"

"After. Maybe twenty or thirty seconds," Egil answered.

"Good. You're not as stupid as you look."

"Was it Black Magic?" Egil asked.

"Worse. It was a demon on the other end of the line. You placed a long distance call to hell." Jake seemed pleased with his jest. "I've seen enough. Let's go back to my shop. I think we could both use a drink."

Jake had pulled out a bottle of Scotch whisky, a much better bottle than Egil was used to drinking, and poured a couple of fingers in each with a splash of water.

"So, you're saying that whoever was on the other end of the phone line conjured a demon?" Egil asked.

"Slange," Jake said. "No, the being on the other end was a demon. There's a big difference. A conjured demon is under some sort of control, which usually implies a demon of the weaker sort. This is a demon acting on his own, for his own purposes. That's much more dangerous."

"Have you ever dealt with a demon before?" Egil asked.

"Once, during the war."

"You were in the war?" Egil asked, not quite sure which war he meant. He had never really established Jake's age, and he was half way afraid he meant the Civil War. Or something older.

"Yes, I was in the war. I volunteered my services right after war was declared. I had friends that were sent to the death camps." The way the old man said it left no doubt in Egil's mind that he was telling the truth. "Here, I'll show you something."

He got up and went into the other room. After a minute he returned with a framed photograph. It showed a handful of men in naval officer's uniforms standing on a dock with what looked like a destroyer as a backdrop. One of the men looked exactly like the man holding the picture.

"Early in the war the navy was desperate. The Nazis were sinking half the ships heading to Europe. I found myself a warrant officer doing convoy duty. If you ever have a chance to travel by destroyer, don't."

"You must have been the oldest man in the service," Egil quipped.

"There was one other older than me in the British army. Colonel Ambrosius. You might know him better by his first name — Merlin." Egil didn't bother to ask if Jake meant *the* Merlin.

"The worst menace that we faced was a U-boat skipper named Manfred von Teufel," Jake continued. "Aptly named. Only the Nazis would employ a demon. He preyed on Allied shipping for months. His wolf pack was responsible for sinking over a hundred ships, and cost the lives of over three thousand men. I was on an escort to one of the convoys he hit. That's when I sensed he was a demon."

"We finally trapped him in the seas between Greenland and Iceland. It took seven wizards acting together on seven precisely positioned ships. Even then it was a close run thing."

"So you destroyed this von Teufel?" Egil asked.

"You don't destroy a demon, but we did banish him from this world for a thousand years. It will be someone else's problem if he returns."

"Do you think you can banish this demon?"

"Maybe, but I'll need to know more about it." Jake answered.

Egil nodded. Both men knew that they would have to try.

As an afterthought Egil asked, "Do you have your discharge papers?"

"Somewhere," Jake answered. "Why?"

"It might help with the other problem. I've got an idea. Something I remember reading once."

They finished the whisky while they made their plans.

When Egil arrived at Jake's the next evening he found the old man pouring over a volume of old maps.

"I'm looking for a place of power that we can use to trap this demon," Jake explained to Egil. "This is a map of mounds erected by the native Indians. They lived on this land a long time before the white man came. They knew the places to draw on the power of the earth, and that's where they built their mounds."

"Have you found a place that will work?" Egil asked.

"I think so. These mounds here," he said pointing to a map in the book. "They are in what is now a nature reserve. That means the mounds will not be disturbed. There won't be people around to get hurt if we should fail. You can see that they form a cross. If we can lure the demon into the where the two lines cross, we may be able to force him back to where he came from."

"Well, you've had better luck than I have," Egil said. I wasn't able to find out much about de Castro. He's a very shadowy figure."

"Do you think you can contact him?" Jake asked.

"I still have the phone number. That seems to be a direct line to him."

"If you could arrange a meeting, maybe use the papers you've been working on as bait. It will be dangerous."

"Not doing anything is dangerous. He's already had my office broken into, and he could have killed me at the phone booth. He's probably figured out that the call was from me."

"Arrange a meeting at this place, then. Sunrise or sunset would be best. And the sooner the better."

"I'll go look for another payphone," Egil said. "I'll let you know as soon as I have it set up."

Egil took the same precautions with the phone as before. He hoped they would be enough. Still, it was with some trepidation that he dialed the number.

When it was answered Egil said, "Don't hang up, de Castro. And don't blow up the phone. I want to cut a deal."

"Mr. Njalsson, is it?" the voice on the other end asked. "What is this deal you want to make, and why should I bother. There are simpler methods to deal with you."

"But we both know those methods are messier and might raise suspicions. I've got the evidence of prior art relating to your patent. The originals. Without them I don't think there can be a successful challenge. I'm willing to turn the papers over to you to get you off my back. That and, say, three thousand dollars so I can take a vacation out of town — if you understand my meaning."

"You read too many detective novels, Mr. Njalsson. And I think two thousand will be sufficient for your vacation."

"Ok. Two thousand. But we meet at a time and place of my choosing."

"You're becoming tedious, Njalsson, but I agree."

Egil told him the place Jake had said and arranged to meet him at sunrise. He hung up and erased his protection, but this time the phone didn't explode.

Jake had told Egil to meet him at the parking lot of the nature reserve an hour before sunrise. Egil had offered to pick him up, but the old man said he had made other arrangements.

When he arrived, the parking lot was empty except for an older Ford station wagon. Egil his car pulled up beside the wagon. Four men were standing around smoking and leaning against the car hood while Jake was waiting at the back. The men at the hood stubbed out their cigarettes and moved to join Jake.

"I brought some colleagues," Jake explained as he greeted Egil. "Their ancestors built the mounds."

As Egil got a closer look at the four in the light of the parking lot's security light he noted that they all appeared to be in their late fifties or early sixties. They were dressed casually, but neatly, in jeans and jackets. They were lean muscular men whose weathered faces indicated a lifetime spent outdoors. Only their high cheek bones and prominent noses marked them as Native Americans.

"You should know," the man who seemed to be their leader said, "that we are only here to restore the balance." The expressions on the faces of the four weren't exactly hostile, but they weren't friendly, either.

"I understand," Egil replied. "We're all here because we have to be."

"Good. That's settled. Shall we get this show on the road, Jacob Far From Home?"

"Do you have what you need?" Jake asked.

"Our stuff is in the bag."

Jake picked up a satchel that had been laying next to the wagon and what looked like the case for a pool cue. He headed down one of the paths into the preserve. Without a word the others followed in single file, with Egil bringing up the rear.

The path lead across a small prairie, through chest high grass. The sky was beginning to lighten in the east, and Egil could make out a low mound off to the side. It was maybe ten feet high, wider at one end and pointed at the other. As they walked, Jake kept looking to either side as if he was trying to get his bearings.

They had gone maybe a hundred yards or so passed the mound when Jake stopped. He looked carefully to the left and right holding out his hand as if it were a pointer.

"Charlie Little Eagle, is this the center?" Jake asked.

The oldest of the four men looked in each direction. Egil could make out the shape of a low hill about fifty yards ahead of them. To either side were small, round mounds. The three mounds along with the one they had passed coming in formed a rough cross. It wasn't something that you'd notice with a casual glance, but it was apparent if you were paying attention. None of the mounds was more than a dozen feet high, just tall enough to stick out above the prairie grass. The two off to the side were circular humps fifteen feet in diameter. The one in front looked like it formed a half moon shape with the open end towards them.

"This is the place," Little Eagle said. He dropped the bag he was carrying and rummaged around in it. He came out with a small drum and beater and a pair of turtle shell rattles. He handed the drum to one of his companions and gave the rattles to the other two. Next he pulled out a long pipe which looked just like a "peace pipe" from a western movie. The bowl was shaped like a hatchet head and an eagle feather hung from the end.

Carefully he filled the bowl of the pipe from a pouch that had hung inside his shirt around his neck. He pulled a lighter from the front pocket of his jacket and lit the pipe, drawing gently on the mouthpiece until the tobacco caught.

He straightened up and faced to the north. Egil noted that the half moon mound was directly in front of him. The drum began to sound with a slow, steady beat. The rattles joined in quietly. Without preamble, Little Eagle chanted a phrase in a language Egil didn't recognize, then took a deep draw from the pipe, exhaling towards the crescent shaped mound. Slowly he turned counter clockwise to face the west and repeated the performance. Once more he turned, this time facing the long mound to the south. Finally, he faced the sunrise and took a last puff.

He then exchanged the pipe for the drum and the drummer performed an identical ritual. Each of the rattle bearers took their turn. After the fourth shaman had finished he returned the pipe to Little Eagle. He handed the pipe to Jake. Jake faced the north repeated the chant and took a puff on the pipe. As far as Egil could tell, he used the same phrase as the others. He repeated the motions to the other three directions, then handed the pipe back to Little Eagle.

"The white man should smoke the pipe as well, Jacob Far From Home. Is his heart pure?"

"I will vouch for his heart," Jake replied.

Little Eagle handed the pipe to Egil.

"I don't know the words." Egil said.

"Just call to the powers of the four winds," Jake said.

Egil hesitated a moment, then holding the pipe to the north called out to the north wind. At the last moment he chose to switch to Old Norse instead of English. He repeated the motions with each of the cardinal directions and then handed the pipe back to Little Eagle, holding it side ways as he had seen the others do.

Little Eagle took the pipe, ground a bare spot on the ground and then tapped out the ashes on it. He put the pipe, the drum, and the rattles back in his bag.

"Hope to see you later, Jacob," he said as he headed to the northern mound. Without a word the other three each headed to one of the other mounds.

"What now? De Castro should be here in a few minutes."

"You stand on the spot where Little Eagle dumped the tobacco. Don't move off that spot. It's all that protects you. I'll go hide in the grass so he doesn't see me."

"And your friends?" Egil asked.

"They will be waiting on the mounds for my signal."

Jake pulled a small pouch from his satchel. It contained a white powder that he spread in a small circle around Egil. It made him feel like the bullseye of a target. Then he ducked off into the grass.

The sun was just popping up over the horizon when Egil saw de Castro coming along the path. He was alone, as they had arranged, but then a demon didn't really need earthly protection.

"You've chosen a strange place to meet, Njalsson."

"I thought it would be better if we did our business without witnesses. I wanted to make sure you were alone."

"I wouldn't need help if I wanted to destroy you. Did you bring what I asked for?"

"No, he didn't."

Jake had popped out of the grass directly behind de Castro. He was holding a short lance with a flint head and had placed himself between the sunrise and the demon. Egil noticed a figure standing on each of the four mounds.

"And who is this old man? This is you little fortune teller, isn't it?" de Castro asked with a smirk. "You shouldn't interfere in things you don't understand, old man."

"I understand more than you think, ——." The last was a name that Egil didn't think a human mouth could pronounce. De Castro looked startled. Jake had called him by his true name.

"Yes, I know who you are. By the powers of the North, West, South and East, by the powers of Earth, Air, Fire and Water. I command you to return to the bowels of hell."

"Who do you think you are, old man?"

Suddenly, from the north Little Eagle cried out. The call was picked up by the shaman on the west mound, then the one on the south, and finally the one on the mound to the east. As the last man finished, Jake lunged at de Castro, the lance held before him. When the point of the lance struck there was a brilliant flash of light that temporarily blinded Egil. He could feel an intense heat and a wind blowing to the place de Castro had occupied. Of de Castro, nothing remained.

When he could see again, Egil noticed that the grass around him was blackened in a circle centered on where de Castro had been standing. Jake was still holding the lance but the flint had shattered.

"You wouldn't have a small nip on you, Egil? I think I could do with a drink."

Egil handed him the small flask he had kept in the breast pocket of his jacket. Jake took a long pull, then handed it back. Egil took a quick drink before restoring it to his pocket.

The four shamans made their way down from the mounds to join them.

"It's done, then?" Little Eagle asked.

"At least for our lifetimes," Jake replied.

"That may be a while, then," Little Eagle said mysteriously.

The four turned and started down the path to the parking lot.

"If you ever need a lawyer, Jake will know how to contact me," Egil called out.

"I'll keep that in mind, Egil Njalsson," Charlie Little Eagle said with a wave of his hand.

"Come. Buy me some breakfast. That's the least you can do," Jake said.

☆　☆　☆　☆　☆

Several weeks went by before Egil saw Jake again. The challenge had been filed against Consolidated Holding's patent. The indications were that they wouldn't contest. Egil was paid for the work he had done on the challenge. Strictly speaking, his actions against the demon de Castro had not been part of his commission, but the client had seen fit to include a five thousand dollar bonus for "services rendered." It wasn't clear how much they knew about the details, but they seemed pleased with the results.

Egil had had some time to deal with other matters which was the reason he visited Jake's shop.

"Egil, good to see you. You don't have another problem, do you?" Jake asked when he entered the shop.

"No, things are just fine. There have been no repercussions following our little outing in the park. I just wanted to return those papers I borrowed. And to give you this."

Jake looked at the paper Egil handed him. "I don't understand. This is a license to practice magic. I didn't apply for this or take a test."

"To be exact, it is a Practitioner's License Third Class. Seeing the picture of you in the Navy jogged something in my memory, something I remembered when I was studying law. There was a clause in the Veteran's Benefits Act of 1946. It was designed to help soldiers and sailors return to civilian life. Anyone who had picked up or used a skill in the service could use that experience to automatically qualify for an entry level government license or certification upon payment of applicable fees. You practiced magic in the Navy; therefore you are entitled to practice magic as a civilian."

"I showed the judge in your case your discharge papers. He was quite sympathetic. It seems he got his law degree on the G.I. Bill. Your rating on your discharge was clearly listed as "Wizard" and the fingerprints matched those on the arrest file. He vacated the judgment against you and ordered the return of the fine. He also expedited the issuance of the license. Incidentally, the fine just covered the application fee."

"I seem to remember that you paid for the fine out of your own pocket," Jake said.

"It turns out to have been a good investment. I got a nice bonus from my client."

"Then it sounds like we both have cause to celebrate. Will you join me for a drink?"

"I'd be happy to."

WIZARD AT LAW

WIZARD AT LAW

☆　☆　☆　☆　☆

He had been sitting with his feet up on the desk when the client came in. The remains of a hamburger from the corner drugstore were sitting on top of the brief that he had been writing, but at that moment he had been listening to the drone of the rain outside his window and staring absently at the words "Egil Njalsson, Attorney" printed backwards on the dirty frosted glass of his office door.

The pose wasn't one to impress a potential client, but then there was little about the office that would impress, anyway. True, there were a pair of framed sheepskins, one from the California Institute of Thaumaturgy and the other from the State University's School of Law, but the paint on the wall they hung from was faded and peeling. A twenty eight year old lawyer in practice by himself couldn't afford much in the way of a luxurious office. Njalsson's was a one room cubicle on the third floor of an aging commercial building.　He shared the building with a passport photographer and a couple of mail order firms. One of the mail order firms was under investigation by the post office for fraud. Egil wouldn't have touched the case for a million dollars. The passport photographer made a little money on the side shooting porn. He sold it to the mail order company.

It didn't look as though the client would be too particular. He wasn't wearing a topcoat, and his jacket was soaked from the rain. It was dirty, too, and one of the pockets had been torn. The man was breathing heavily, not surprisingly so, as the elevator hadn't worked in two months, but there was a weariness about his eyes; a sunkenness about his cheekbones that spoke of a prolonged period of exertion.

Njalsson let the man catch his breath while he sized him up. The jacket was of good quality, though worn. Possibly the man was just fond of the garment, or else simply careless of his appearance, but it might also mean that while he might have had money once, he was currently on hard times. Of course, he might have gotten it in a second hand shop that same day. Egil sighed. People with money didn't come to young lawyers without reputations, not in that neighborhood and not at nine o'clock at night.

As he waited, Egil noted something else about the man. He was scared. Not fright or a crazy fear, but he had the look of a man who was watching helplessly while his world unraveled about him. Finally, the man pulled himself together and between labored breaths asked, "Are you Njalsson the lawyer?"

He didn't sound like a wino. His voice was terse, as if he were used to being respected, used to giving orders. "Yes, I am," Egil replied. "What can I do for you, Mr. —?"

The man ignored his query and turned to close the door. As he did so some of the hunted look left him. He took a seat in the wooden chair facing the desk. "I need help — legal help."

"Well, that's what I'm here for," Egil answered. He wasn't sure whether the man would be able to pay anything, but he was bored with the brief he had been working on. He'd at least hear the man out. "I'll need to know some of the details first of course. Why don't you start by telling me who you are."

"Fredericks, George Fredericks." When he saw that the name didn't register he added, "I own Fredericks' Paraphernalia."

The name suddenly rang a bell, but it didn't seem to fit the man sitting across the desk from me. Fredericks' Paraphernalia wasn't a big company, not like General Magic or International Divination Apparatus, but it did have a reputation for being on the leading edge of technology. There were subtle things like notes in the trade magazines and government research contracts. If the man was telling the truth, there was no question about his ability to pay — not unless the market had crashed while Egil had been working.

Fredericks must have noted the suspicion on Njalsson's face. "Look, I don't have much time. They're after me. Will you take the case?"

"Exactly who is after you, Mr. Fredericks?" He didn't like the edginess that seemed to have taken hold of the other man. His ears had pricked up as though they had heard something, something that disturbed him. Egil began to wonder if the man was a paranoid. All he needed at the moment was a psychotic for a client.

"The police," Fredericks said, matter of factly. "They've been after me since yesterday. I didn't go home last night. That's why I look this way."

"Just what do they want you for?"

"Murder. They said that I killed a woman."

Egil raised his eyebrows. Murders by wealthy industrialists were a little outside his experience. "Did you?"

"No, but they have enough evidence to prove that I did. That's why I need a lawyer."

"But why me, Mr. Fredericks? Certainly a man like you must already have lawyers," Egil said.

"I'm not sure that I can trust them. Besides, I haven't been able to get in touch with them and I need one now. I saw your window from the street and the light. I'm desperate. I've got to talk to someone before they get me."

"Thanks. I'm glad you've got confidence in my ability," Egil remarked wryly.

"Look. Here's two hundred dollars. It's all I have on me. Will you take the case?"

The bills were crisp and green, tens and twenties. The rent was due in a week and Egil's bank account held eleven dollars and twenty three cents. "You've got yourself a lawyer, Mr. Fredericks."

He was about to say more, but the wail of a siren sounded outside on the street. The flashing red lights reflected across the ceiling of the office. Fredericks stiffened at the sound and looked desperately at the door. He half rose from the chair, but the energy seemed to have drained from his body. He slumped back in resignation.

"If they are after you, I wouldn't advise trying to get away. At least not in my professional capacity. It wouldn't look good. If they arrest you, I'll try to get you out on bail."

"Whatever you say. I'm tired of running. When you bail me out, just make sure that it's me."

Egil didn't have time to figure out the last remark. The sounds of flat feet were echoing in the stairwell. There were at least three of them. They seemed to know what they were about, too. They came directly to the office. Egil could see a form silhouetted against the glass. They didn't bother to knock.

A beefy cop in uniform opened the door, but it was the two plain clothes men who entered first. Njalsson could see how they had been so sure of themselves in tracking down Fredericks. One of the detectives was short and dark, and the hat on his head didn't quite conceal the points of his ears. Egil looked down at his hands for confirmation and saw the thick mat of dark hair on the palms that indicated a lycanthrope. They must have wanted Fredericks badly to have assigned a werewolf to the case. True lycanthropic talents were rare, and of those who did have the werewolf's ability to sniff out the trail of a fugitive, a trait of insanity made most useless for police work. This one appeared to be a borderline case. He seemed half ready to attack. Probably useless during a full moon, Njalsson thought to himself.

The other detective addressed Fredericks, pointedly ignoring Njalsson. "You've caused us a lot of trouble, Fredericks. Don't give me any excuses." The uniformed cop was moving forward with his handcuffs.

"There's no need to use that tone. I've already advised my client to surrender himself voluntarily," Egil said. His statement wasn't quite accurate, but he always allowed himself a little legal license. "I don't think that there is any need for restraint."

"I'll decide that," the detective said nodding to the uniform to go ahead. The bracelets snapped shut with a sharp snick. The cop seemed to be enjoying himself. "Just who are you, anyway? Maybe I should take you in as an accessory."

It was clear that Egil was messing up what they had hoped would be a nice, clean collar. Maybe Fredericks had been right in fearing the police. The werewolf was standing off to the side, his lips parted to reveal prominent, pointed canines. He was salivating, too, Egil noted, the hair on his own neck stiffening. He had had contact with shapestrong people before, but he had never liked the experience. The animal nature in them was too close to the surface. He wondered if Fredericks would have made it to the station alive if he hadn't come into the picture. But with a lawyer as a witness, they couldn't really pull any fast ones.

"I'd advise against that. Mr. Fredericks has retained me as counsel in this matter. If you try to interfere with our attorney client relationship you may find yourself with a suit for false arrest. And just for the record, I'd like to have your name and badge number."

Egil wanted the detective to understand just where he stood. A sixth sense told him that there were some big powers behind the frame up, if that was what it was. He didn't want anything to happen to his client before he could bail him out. He was pushing them, he knew, but it looked as though all these cops would understand was pushing.

The head cop gave him a dirty look, but he produced his badge. Njalsson had messed up his game, but the cop had enough experience to not make trouble for himself. He'd let others, higher up, do the worrying. Egil jotted the numbers and names down on the wrappings of his hamburger.

The wallet snapped shut in his face and the detective jerked his thumb at the door. The cop and the werewolf started out, Fredericks pinioned between them. By the time Egil had finished writing down the names, they were halfway to the stairs. He had time only to blurt out instructions to Fredericks not to say anything before he watched his client disappear down the stairs.

It was too late to see a judge about bail that night, and the chances were that they would shuffle him around most of the night just to keep him from talking to Njalsson. The lawyer had been skeptical at first, but the cops had been too quick in hustling Fredericks away. He would have been more sure of himself if it had been a good, clean collar. Detectives didn't come cheap, and Egil had a hunch that at least a captain had been bought, maybe even higher.

Fredericks wasn't a pauper, either. If it was a frame, and it had all the earmarks of one, there was big money involved. The question was, who's? He wondered if he wasn't getting in a bit over his head. But he had taken Frederick's money, and he wasn't the kind to back down.

There wasn't much that he could do to spring Fredericks at that hour of the night, but at least he could start getting some background information. Fredericks hadn't had much of a chance to fill him in. In fact, Egil didn't even know who it was that Fredericks was supposed to have murdered. Luckily, he had his own contacts in the police department, though they could be bought for the price of a beer.

He dumped the remains of the hamburger in the waste basket and crumpled the wrapping with the detective's name and badge number into his jacket pocket. The brief could wait. It might be a couple of months before he would get paid for that. He had two hundred in his pocket and he might as well start to earn it.

It was still raining when he got outside, and he cursed himself for forgetting his hat. It was a bad night to be chasing around, but when, he thought, was there a good one? He pulled his collar up against the cold April rain and got into his car.

The best place to start would be Al's. The diner wasn't far from the station and Egil knew some of the cops that ate there. As there had probably been an APB out on Fredericks, he would be able to pick up some of the details when some of his friends came off their shift.

It was 10:30 — a little early — leaving Egil half an hour until the shifts changed. He bought a paper and ordered a cup of coffee and a sandwich to pass the time. He'd been busy on the brief and hadn't seen a paper in a couple of days. There might even be something on Fredericks in there.

There was. He saw it as he opened the front page. Over a typically gory crime photograph was the headline "Industrialist Arrested in Mutilation Murder."   Another, smaller picture was recognizable as Fredericks. They hadn't wasted any time on this one. In fact, he was reading the eight o'clock edition which had been on the streets an hour before Fredericks had showed up in his office.

He read further to find out the details. Whoever had planned the frame had had a good imagination. The victim, one Diane Friendly, had been found in her apartment by a neighbor, her body separated into several pieces. Naturally, the apartment turned out to have been rented by one George Fredericks who had often been seen in the company of the victim. Witnesses had been found who had seen the two having a fight in a restaurant earlier on the evening of the murder.

Circumstantially, it was damning as hell, Egil thought, but the story carried no details of the arrest, only the fact that the suspect had been apprehended.   That wasn't surprising considering the problem in timing.   The story must have been prepared before hand, or the police had given out bad information. But that meant that they had been awfully sure of themselves. No wonder the cops had been so upset with his own involvement. They might have trouble explaining it to a judge, provided he could prove Fredericks had been in his office at nine.

He wondered how Fredericks had gotten mixed up with the Friendly broad. The little man didn't look the type. Egil knew her by reputation, though not personally. She wasn't the type to run in the circles frequented by starving lawyers. She had been a good looking woman, and had used her looks to run with the money.   Maybe she had been attracted by Fredericks's wealth, but there might be more to it. He'd have to check into it.

He was interrupted by a hulking shape in blue that grabbed the stool next to him at the counter. "Reading up on the latest gore, counselor? I'd thought you'd be out chasing ambulances."

"The weather's too rotten to go after ambulances," Egil replied when he recognized his friend, O'Neil. "How many tickets did you fix today, Joe?"

Pointing at the paper he asked, "What's the word on this one?"

"Nasty business," the cop said shaking his head. "I know the man that answered the first call. He said that he puked his guts out when he saw it, and he'd been in the army in Co chin. Too bad about the doll. From what you can see in the paper, she was a real good looker. Why the interest?"

"I'm defending Fredericks," Njalsson said noncommittally.

"Better find yourself a good shrink, then. Your only hope is to prove that he's funny in the head."

"Why do you say that?"

"It doesn't say so in the paper, but they've got two eye witnesses who saw Fredericks going into the place just before they heard the girl scream. He came out half an hour later and there was blood on his clothing. The identification was pretty positive, so I don't see how you can beat the rap on this one."

"Sounds pretty bad," Egil admitted. "Well, at least he's got the money to pay my fee. A nice murder won't hurt my reputation even if I lose."

O'Neil was a friend, but Egil didn't know for sure how far he could trust him. He didn't want the opposition to get a hint of his suspicions. It looked as though he was facing big enough hurdles as it was.

"You're all heart, counselor, but that Fredericks guy is loaded all right. Wonder what makes a guy like that do such a thing. He didn't look that fierce when they brought him in. Puny little fellow, too. You wouldn't think he had the strength."

"You saw them bring him in?"

"Yeah, it was about seven. But you must know that."

"Sure. Well, I've got to get going."

"Yeah, me too. The wife's expecting me. See you." The big cop got up, forgetting to pay for his coffee. Egil plunked down a buck and followed, stuffing the rest of his sandwich into his mouth.

Things were looking curiouser and curiouser as the saying went. According to O'Neil, Fredericks had been brought in at seven. Strangely enough, Fredericks had been sitting in his own office nearly two hours later when he was arrested. Egil was just beginning to realize how big the magic in the case was.

☆   ☆   ☆   ☆   ☆

It was a long dreary drive to the apartment where the girl had lived. The rain came down in sheets against the windshield, and his headlights were two dim yellow tunnels in the dark. The heater in his car didn't work, and he shivered as he drove.

The apartment was across town up in the foothills — not a neighborhood usually bothered by crime. The houses that he passed on the winding road were set well back from the street and had a tendency to be hidden behind walls or hedges. Egil managed to get lost in the dark and it was nearly one before he pulled past the place.

Whatever the relationship between Friendly and his client had been, Fredericks had not been cheap. The rent on the apartment must have been three grand a month at least. The swimming pool off to the side had a climate spell on it, a type of magic classed as conspicuous consumption. Someplace down in Florida or California there was a corresponding area where it snowed in the winter while at pool side it was in the eighties. Even now, for a circle of twenty yards around the pool, the decking and grass were high and dry despite the rain. That sort of thing took a first class climate wizard, not to mention the rent on the land at the other end of the spell — though on second thought, if you were smart you could probably sell the rainfall to some California truck farmer for irrigation.

Egil had seen a cop on the front door, so he drove past and parked around the corner. A little checking showed that the pool side door hadn't been secured. He let himself in. After orienting himself in the building he headed for the girl's apartment. Unfortunately, a guard had been posted there as well, and his threats and credentials weren't impressive enough to get past the cop. For a moment he thought about using some of the two hundred to bribe the man, but then thought better of it. If the man could be bought, he was facing somebody with more capital. Besides, he had gotten part of what he needed.

There was something rotten going on; Egil was convinced of that. He wasn't a witch smeller. Like lycanthropy, that was more a matter of heredity than training. He had been tested for the ability when a student at CalThaum and been found lacking. But there were things even a layman could sense if the scent was strong enough. He had smelled it outside the door of Diane Friendly's apartment. The odor of magic had been thick and heavy. There had been a lacing of Brimstone in it, too. That meant that whoever had made the frame was in league with the darker powers. The game was being played for high stakes.

Egil decided to get out of there before the cop got too annoyed or suspicious. He wasn't going to get any more out of the cop and he had other sources of information, anyway. He turned around the way he had come and headed back to his car.

On the way he passed the door to the underground garage. There was a possibility that the lab boys hadn't bothered with it. There really wasn't any need as the murder had occurred upstairs. But there was a chance that he might find something useful.

The garage had the usual assortment of Mercedes', BMW's, and Cadillacs that went with the rent bracket. There were at least thirty cars parked in the garage, but by luck, some helpful building superintendent had painted the apartment number by each place. It didn't take Egil long to find the white Mercedes two seater that had belonged to Diane Friendly. The doors were locked, but a former client who was serving three to five had shown him how to circumvent such obstacles. It didn't involve any magic, either, just a piece of spring steel.

He used his handkerchief as he rummaged through the car so as not to leave any fingerprints or aura. He wasn't quite sure what he was looking for, so Egil just started poking. The glove compartment contained the typical collection of feminine artifacts, none of which looked as though they would be of use. Just to be thorough he felt around underneath the seats and came up with a reward, an address book. He stuffed in into his pocket for later examination. For good measure he pocketed the pair of sunglasses that he found on the dash. He'd need them at his next stop. Carefully he closed the door, wiping it before returning to his car.

Egil knew his own limitations. While he had picked up a good grounding in magic during his studies at CalThaum before going into law, he was familiar only with those principles involving the Half World, the so called "white" and "green" magics. Contact with the Dark World, what had once been called "black magic", was forbidden by law, and information on the subject was purposefully limited. He was out of his league knowing almost nothing of the techniques involved, but he did know one man who might have the knowledge needed to prove Fredericks' innocence.

It was a good thing that Old Jack kept unusual hours, for by the time Njalsson reached the rundown shop it was approaching three in the morning. There was a light in the window, however, so he let himself in through the front door. The bell overhead jingled to announce his presence, but it was hard to say whether the old man could hear it over the scratchy music of the hand cranked Victrola that he was listening to. In any case, Old Jack paid him no attention, nor would he until the record had finished playing.

To all appearances, the shop was a second hand store, but Egil doubted that much had been sold in the last twenty years. Instead, the proprietor made his living with a modest but illegal trade in fortune telling and odd bits of magic. The antiques provided a front, but beyond that, Old Jack just felt comfortable with them. Egil had never been able to get two consistent accounts of the old man's age, but there could be no doubt that he was a man from another, simpler era.

Egil had made his acquaintance when the court had appointed him to defend the old man for practicing without a license. Jack had never had any formal schooling, and he steadfastly refused to take any of the exams necessary to obtain a license, claiming that he knew more than the examiners. There was a good deal of truth in the remark, but that had not weighed heavily with the court. Egil had lost the case, but his efforts had won the friendship or at least the tolerance of his client. Since then, the lawyer had found the old man a useful source of information and magical lore, and he had proved of help in several cases.

The record came to an end, and the old man carefully lifted the needle and placed the record back in a stack to the side of the antique machine. When he finally looked up, Egil reached into his pocket and pulled out a pint of Irish whiskey. Jack took it eagerly and, breaking the seal, took a long pull lowering the level of the amber liquid by a good two fingers.

As he watched him drink, Egil tried for the hundredth time to figure the old man out. While his information on magic was invariably detailed and correct, Jack was vague about his own personal history. Not that he wasn't willing to tell a story, but they never seemed to agree. He had on various occasions claimed to be a gypsy, a Hindu swami, a Finnish sorcerer, a defrocked priest, a rabbi, and a druid. He had even claimed to be a Yaqui brujo once when he had been very, very drunk, going so far as to recite a prayer to the Great Spirit in what he had claimed was his native tongue. With each story, Jack would lapse into the suitable dialect. His Latin and Hebrew were flawless as far as Egil could tell, but that did nothing to clarify the issue. He had once seen a Victorian vintage photograph hanging on Jack's wall that showed a group of somber men with long beards and hair standing in front of a Polish synagogue. One of the men bore at least a superficial resemblance to Jack, allowing for time, but then, he had also seen a familiar face in a Daguerreotype showing a gypsy wagon. In either case the resemblance might well be coincidental, leaving Jack's antecedents as much a mystery as ever. That didn't prevent Egil from wondering.

"Ah, you're a good lad for a Sassenach, Egil, even with your heathen name," Jack said in a brogue to fit his beverage. "What can I be doing to repay this liquid kindness? Your fortune told to find out when you'll land a big client? Or maybe a wee drop of a potion to help you seduce some lovely young lass?"

"I'm here on business. I need some help on a case that I've got. I think someone is trying to frame a client of mine by using magic, but I'm not familiar enough with the techniques being used to prove it."

"Would ye be havin' me practice the Art without a license now counselor? Ye of all people should know better. Ye defended me yerself when the judge gave me ninety days or ninety dollars. And me an old man without a farthing to me name."

"And who ended up paying the fine?" Egil asked, not that he regretted the ninety bucks. It had paid off well as an investment. He had also gotten the verdict vacated on a technicality and had obtained a license for Jack, which the old man had since let lapse as being useless.

"As your lawyer I wouldn't advise you to do anything illegal. But I think that I might persuade my client to acquire some antiques. Say fifty dollars now and another hundred dollars worth later. And if you might want to tell me some tall tales, well what's the harm in that. Now that doesn't sound illegal, does it?"

"You're a shyster alright, lad, and a pirate, too. Just like your Viking ancestors. But I'm always willing to put one over on the Excise men. Now take that vase over there. Pretty thin it be. Worth fifty dollars wouldn't you say?" He gave a conspiratorial wink and took another three fingers off the bottle. 'But a hundred and fifty, that's a bit higher than you're normally wont to pay for what I know." The old man was suddenly more than just a drunk.

Egil outlined what he knew, both from the papers, and from what O'Neil had told him. Old Jack listened carefully without interruption until Egil came to his investigation at the victim's apartment.

"Describe the smell to me. Exactly now. Don't leave anything out," he said sharply. "And leave the interpretations to me."

"There was brimstone, burning sulfur," Egil answered. "And almonds, too. And a hint of something sickeningly sweet."

"Rotten fruit — did you smell rotten fruit?" the warlock asked testily.

"Yes, that could be it. I really don't have the nose for this kind of work. But it could have been rotten fruit."

"Mark me well, laddy. That's what it was, alright. If what you say is true, then there would have had to have been the smell of rotten fruit. It's not the sort of thing they teach you in them fancy technical schools, but any hedge gypsy worth the name could tell you as much. And it's not something I like."

"But what was it? What does the smell mean?" Egil asked.

"It's the smell of a demon, a denizen of the Dark World."

"Was that what killed the girl — a demon?"

"What killed the girl was simulacrum, a replica of your client. There's nothing inherently evil in such, nor are they difficult to conjure up. Advertising men use them often. So do jewelers, though in that case it is an object and not a person they duplicate." As he talked, the brogue had left Jack's voice, and it took on a pedantic tone.

"Of course such constructs have no real existence, being but illusions. But you can put such a seeming on an object and animate it, too, if you can find a spirit that's willing. But to kill, and purposefully. There's only one place such a spirit could be found, and that's the Dark World."

"Dealing with the Dark Powers," Egil said, disbelievingly. He had half suspected as much, but had not been willing to accept the possibility as real. "Not only is that grossly illegal, but I know enough about magic to know how dangerous that can be."

After a pause he added, "And what price must be paid." Selling a soul was not a piece of fiction as the aftermath of the last world war had proved.

"Do you have perhaps something from the room where the girl was murdered?" Jack asked. "This is strong magic, and such often leaves a residue on things nearby. It might be possible to learn who your client's enemies are."

Egil explained how the apartment had been guarded, preventing his entry. "Too bad," the old man said, shaking his head. "It might mean the difference between saving him or not. It is dangerous to operate blind in these circumstances."

"I couldn't get into her apartment, but I did get into her car," Egil said, trying to be helpful. "I pocketed these just in case they might be useful." He pulled the address book and the sunglasses from his pocket. He knew that an adept could often gain impressions of a person from objects that they had worn or handled frequently. He was counting on Old Jack's ability in that art to give his investigation some direction.

The old man smiled at him. "You did well. You've got the instinct. You might have made a good wizard if that fancy technical school hadn't given you all the wrong ideas."

"It's a funny thing about glasses, you know," the old man said as he took the case from Egil. "They are like a person's own eyes. Everything that the wearer sees, he sees through the glasses. It can leave an impression, too, just like a finger print, if the wearer is in the right frame of mind. Why don't we see just what we can see."

Very carefully, Old Jack removed the glasses from their case using his thumb and forefinger and holding them so that he touched only the frames. There was nothing of the old drunk about him now. He was moving with all the skill and precision of a jeweler. Gently he laid them out on the top of a small table that was covered with black velvet. Normally, the table served for the laying out of the cards during fortune telling sessions, but Egil had seen it put to other uses on occasion. Now it was to be the stage for the old man's skrying.

The lights were turned off except for one sputtering candle of white bee's wax. Jack began to weave his spell. There were few preliminaries and none of the mumbo jumbo that the old man used with his more gullible clients, only a muted muttering in a language that Egil recognized as Romany, though he did not know enough of it to follow the words. His own training had been in the formal languages of Latin, Greek, Hebrew, and Sanskrit. Gypsy lore was looked down on as being unscientific at best.

Egil had long since left any such prejudices behind. He had seen Jack work far too often to have any doubts about his ability. Now he realized that he was witnessing yet another manifestation of that talent. Of course, it was a well established principle of forensic thaumaturgy that objects at the scene of a crime might retain some impression of that crime if the object had been in close contact with either the victim or the perpetrator. Murder weapons, in particular, often could provide clues. The phenomena had its basis in both the Laws of Sympathetic and Symbolic Magic. But normally, such impressions were left only by the extreme trauma of the moment, and then only when direct physical contact was involved. What Jack was attempting was work of another order entirely.

As Egil watched, the glasses began to glow with a light of their own, and if he looked out through them he could see an image, just as if he were looking through the lenses. The effect was not unlike that used by carnival charlatans with their crystal balls, but Egil was sure it was not a trick.

"Ah, we've got something now, lad," Jack said, obviously excited. He took a quick pull on the bottle without looking at it. "Now I ask. Who killed you, Diane Friendly? Who caused you to be dead?"

The scene in the lenses changed to focus on the head and shoulders of a man. He was middle aged with a swarthy complexion and features that were vaguely Slavic. He was dressed respectably except for a heavy black moustache and he looked like nothing so much as a prosperous businessman.

"Do you know him?"

"No, I've never seen him before," Egil answered. "It's certainly not Fredericks. I wish he were here. He might be able to tell us something. Maybe it's one of his competitors."

"Well, we can do better. We have the book, remember. Perhaps I can give you a name to go with the face." He placed the address book in front of the glassed so that they could read the pages through the lenses. "Give us a name, the name of your killer," he commanded.

Slowly he turned the pages one by one. None of the pages looked notable. They had worked their way through to the S's before it happened. Then one name, Vincent Starenko, was written in blood red ink. Egil could swear that he saw drops flowing from the neat script in which it was written. Yet when he picked the book up to examine it, the name was written in the same black as the others. Only when viewed through the glasses did the name appear red.

"There is your murderer. Vincent Starenko caused the death of the girl."

"This is good, Jack. Better than I had hoped. Now all I have to do is prove it." Evidence produced by magical means was inadmissible in court, a holdover from the superstitious days before modern science had proved the basis for such manifestations. Old Jack's work certainly wouldn't be recognized by any court, but at least he had some leads to go on.

Jack turned the lights back on and carefully placed the glasses back in their case. "Why don't you hang on to them, keep them safe," Egil yawned as he looked at his watch. "It's almost seven, time I started thinking about springing Fredericks. Thanks for your help, Jack. I'll try and get the money to you as soon as possible."

"Egil," the old man said. "Be careful. These are the Dark Powers you deal with. Remember that they have already killed once. More blood is as nothing to them. Guard yourself well."

"I will," Egil said as he left the shop. The rain had stopped and the sun was already peeking through the clouds. He was making some progress on the case and that made him feel good. Now all that he had to do was get down to the station and make arrangements for Fredericks's bail. But first he'd stop off at the farmers' market and get some wolfbane just in case that hardnosed detective and his were friend were waiting for him at the precinct house. Better get some garlic, too, he thought, just in case. As he headed towards his car he was whistling.

☆   ☆   ☆   ☆   ☆

It took Egil almost an hour and a half to get in to see Fredericks, but then that was what he had expected. The wait was ameliorated, though, by the sight of the werewolf's reaction to the wolfbane the lawyer carried in his pocket. The detective's nose had started to run almost immediately, and he had developed an urge to scratch his side with his leg. He had finally been forced to withdraw looking most unhappy. His partner had murder in his eye, but Egil knew his rights.

When they finally escorted him into the interview room, Fredericks was looking more tired and worn than ever. He had not had an easy night. Egil noted that his jacket now bore brownish stains on the sleeves. He also noted that the pocket was no longer torn. Somehow during the night the jacket had been switched for one that bore incriminating evidence. The framers were being very thorough.

When Fredericks saw him his eyes brightened and he started to speak, but Egil signaled silence with his hand. Lawyer client communications were supposedly sacrosanct, but even honest cops had been known to eavesdrop to improve the chances of conviction. Not that the legal profession was without countermeasures. Taking a piece of chalk from his pocket, Egil began to draw three circles around Fredericks and himself. Each one of the rings he closed with an elaborate flourish and inscribed with runes. Hebrew and Greek were more common in spell work, but he preferred the Norse characters, partly because of his ancestry and partly because the lore was more obscure and for that reason harder to defeat.

Fredericks raised his eyebrow quizzically as he watched Egil's handiwork. "I want to keep this conversation confidential. There are a couple of detectives out there who wouldn't mind bending the rules a bit to listen in."

"Pretty good technique for a lawyer," Fredericks observed. "Not exactly the sort of thing they cover in pre-law, is it?"

"I got my bachelor's at CalThaum in applied metaphysics. It wasn't until I graduated in the middle of the aerospace bust that I thought about going into law. I thought I could make more money as a lawyer than as an unemployed aerospace wizard. Sometimes I'm not so sure."

Fredericks seemed to relax a bit at the professional talk. It was clear that his opinion of Njalsson had gone up with the knowledge of his background. He gave the lawyer an approving look and then asked, "Well?"

"There's no doubt that you're being framed," Egil replied, "and in a big way. I checked out the scene of the crime and some other details. As far as I've been able to determine, the crime was committed by a simulacrum animated by a demon."

Fredericks mulled the lawyer's words over for a few moments. From the expression on his face it was clear that he realized their implication. "A demon. That doesn't seem possible. That would mean dealing with the Dark World, and you must be aware of what that means."

"Quite, but what else could kill so wantonly? Certainly not a denizen of the Half World. Besides, I have confirmation from a man that I consider an expert."

"Yes, I agree. You must be right, but it is almost unthinkable. Who would be willing to pay such a price?" Fredericks asked shaking his head.

"Greed is a powerful motivation," Egil answered. "As to whom, I don't know, but I've got some clues. The problem now, though, is that they've got the makings of an airtight frame. The demon that killed the girl was witnessed and arrested in your form. The simulacrum was brought in and booked before seven yesterday, two hours before you were picked up in my office. We might be able to use that against them, but right now it's my word against a couple of dozen cops, and I'm afraid that I'm a biased witness. By the way, to show you how thorough they're being, that jacket is not the one you had on last night. It was worn by the demon. The stains on the sleeves are blood."

Fredericks looked down at his coat, horror widening his eyes. "But you know what happened. Can you get me out?"

"Don't rush things. I said that I knew what happened, not that I could prove it in a court of law. As far as the D. A. is concerned, he's got an open and shut case against you. Witnesses, threatening remarks, even incriminating physical evidence," Egil said, pointing to the jacket where Fredericks had laid it on the table. "I don't know if the D. A. has been bought or not, but with a case like this, it's going to take a lot of persuading to keep him from prosecuting, even if he is honest."

"Don't look so glum. I said that I can't prove it yet, but give me some time. Also, I should be able to get you out on bail, though you'll have to give me power of attorney so that I can arrange the bond. It'll cost you a bundle, but I think that you'll be safer out of here. I don't trust the people who run this joint."

"Of course, whatever you say. You've done quite a lot in the time that you've had, I guess." Fredericks said conciliatorily. "But I still don't understand why. Who could be doing this to me?"

"I might have some idea on the latter. A friend of mine has some peculiar talents. Does the name Vincent Starenko mean anything to you?"

"He works for American Alchemical. He calls himself a troubleshooter, but he's actually more of a hatchet man.

I've had trouble with him before with industrial espionage," Fredericks answered.

"Any reason your girlfriend, Diane Friendly, should have his name in her address book?"

Egil could see that he had struck a nerve with that one. Fredericks was silent for some time before answering. "I suspected her of passing information about my work to someone. That's what the argument was about at the restaurant. I had accused her of it. She denied any involvement, of course, but, well, I had proof."

"I should have known better. I'm not much of a man, not for that kind of a woman. I'm not even that rich, not by the standards she was used to. But she was so beautiful and so loving. Oh, god, why did they have to kill her?"

For a moment Egil thought that Fredericks was going to break down in front of him. "They killed her because she could implicate them. Also, it was a convenient way to get at you."

It sounded cold and hard to Egil's ears, but it was the truth. The opposition was playing for high stakes. Fredericks saw it too, and he pulled himself together, though there was a half insane coldness to his expression.

"I've got to ask you this," Egil said. "Just what were you working on that could be so important?"

Fredericks went stony, eyeing the lawyer suspiciously.

"Look, whatever you say to me is protected by our attorney client relationship. And let's face it; if you can't trust me, you're sunk. It would help me a lot if I knew what it was they were after."

"Alright, I'll tell you. I've discovered a way to degauss iron, to make it amenable to magical manipulations."

Njalsson whistled. It was suddenly clear to him why Starenko and his employers were willing to play the stakes they had been. From time immemorial, the fact that cold iron and steel were inviolate barriers to magic had been one of the basic principles of the Art. That was why jail cells were made out of that metal and people put horseshoes above their doors. No spell could enter a room guarded by iron, nor could magic be used to escape from iron bars. Magic was as powerless against ferrous materials as it was helpless on consecrated ground. It also placed severe limits on the use of magic in industrial processes. The Art was restricted to materials of inferior properties such as bronze or aluminum. Fredericks' discovery was potentially worth millions.

"Diane had stolen my equations and passed them on to Starenko. It won't do them any good, though. I've already applied for the patents, and there is no way around them. I've made sure of that."

"But what if you were out of the way?" Egil asked. "They might stop the application, or have the patents reassigned. That's why they want you out of the picture."

Fredericks nodded grimly.

"Look, I've got to see a judge about springing you. I've got to get going if I'm to get you out of here today." As he erased the circles he couldn't decide whether Fredericks looked forlorn or angry. It was hard to tell with the man's mousey countenance.

On his way out of the station, Egil saw neither the werewolf nor his partner, which made him feel good. He was beginning to get a handle on the case, and for the first time he thought that he had a good chance of pulling Fredericks' chestnuts out of the fire. And if he did pull it off, he'd be in the big money. The case was getting a lot of publicity.

He got into his car and started to drive down to the courthouse to arrange Fredericks' bail, but as he was driving he realized that he was no longer alone. His earlier euphoria came crashing down. Sitting next to him was a thin, dark man, neat and with an impeccable moustache above his narrow lips, but with cold, cruel eyes of an almost transparent blue. Egil became uncomfortably aware of a hard metal tube pressing into his ribs. A quick, sideways glance showed him that his passenger was holding a small but very efficient looking gun on him.

"Just keep driving, Njalsson. All I want to do is talk. For the moment."

Egil was in no position to argue and made a pointed effort to keep his eyes on the road. The rear view mirror showed that they were being followed by a large, black car. It also revealed, or rather failed to reveal something else. The man sitting next to him did not cast a reflection. At first Egil thought it might be some trick of angles, but he knew better than that. He could see the back of the seat and depression his passenger was making in it. The thin, neat man in the dark suit was a demon, one of the denizens of the Dark World.

"Yes, Mr. Njalsson, I am a demon. I trust that shows you just how serious my employers are." Egil nodded. He could feel the sweat building up in his arm pits.

"My employers are not happy about your interference in this case. They think it wise that your relationship with Mr. Fredericks terminate in one manner or another. The choice, of course, is yours."

As he drove, Egil was desperately searching his stock of lore for some counter to the demon. He was beginning to realize the inadequacies of his education. The Dark World and all knowledge of it were under interdict. By law, no citizen could have dealings with it. And it was a law that was seldom broken, not for fear of the legal penalties of this world, but for fear of the far more remorseless laws of the other plane.   But it was the law of this land that had left him defenseless.

"You are not to think that my employers' have any prejudices against you, Mr. Njalsson. It's just that you are, shall we say, an inconvenience. They realize that you stand to gain from this case, and they see no need for you to suffer financially. They are wealthy men, and wealthy men always need lawyers. If you drop the case, I have been instructed to tell you that a certain measure of business will be thrown your way. Quite lucrative business, too, I believe. Think it over.   No need to inform us.   The act will be sufficient."

Suddenly the pressure on his rib cage vanished and when he mustered the courage to look over the gun had disappeared. "You can drop me off along here. Good day, Mr. Njalsson."

Egil did as he was instructed and watched the demon enter the black car which had pulled up behind him.   He tried to catch the license plate number, but curiously, the figures on the plate seemed to shift and change like a mirage. He wasn't sure what he would have done with the number, anyway.

The experience had left Egil shaken, there could be no doubt of that, but it had not changed his plans. He tried to rationalize his decision by thinking that there was no safety in dealing with the Dark Powers on any terms, but the root of his choice was that he hated to have anyone, in this world or any other, tell him what to do. That was why he was a starving lawyer with an almost nonexistent practice instead of a junior partner in a more prosperous firm. One thing was certain, though. In the future he would have to be more careful.

☆   ☆   ☆   ☆   ☆

He had surprisingly little trouble at the courthouse. Perhaps Starenko hadn't considered the possibility that he would go so far, or maybe he had not seen the need to buy that deeply into the legal system. With the case against Fredericks, it didn't appear as though there was much the industrialist could do once free.

It still took the better part of the afternoon for him to arrange all the details. A hundred thousand dollars bail was enough to keep the D.A. happy, though he made the pro forma protests against leaving a psychopathic killer out in public. The judge recognized the prosecutor's arguments for what they were. By the time the bail hearing was held at three, Egil had used Fredericks' power of attorney to obtain the bond. The proceedings themselves were a mere formality.

He went down to the jail to pick up Fredericks, minus, the attorney noted, the bogus jacket he had worn earlier. Doubtless it had now been retained as evidence with the incriminating stains. With the case that he had, it was no wonder that the prosecutor had been confident.

"I was beginning to think that you had forgotten me," Fredericks said as they walked to the car.

"Arranging bail for murder takes time. Besides, I had other things to occupy my time," Fredericks looked at him quizzically. "I'll give you the details later. Right now there's someone I want you to meet. I think that we can prove a simulacrum was used to frame you, but we're going to need some help establishing our case."

Fredericks wasn't at all happy when they pulled up in front of Old Jack's second hand shop. "What are we doing here, Njalsson? I thought that you were taking me to some sort of expert."

"Just how much do you know about the Dark World, Mr. Fredericks?" Egil asked. He was annoyed by the man's tone.

Despite his mild appearance, Fredericks was hard and demanding underneath.

"Well, nothing, really, other than the fact of its existence and some counter spells to prevent the entrance into this world. All our dealings are with the Half World and various nature spirits and elementals. You, as a lawyer, must know that contact with the Dark World is illegal."

"Exactly. As you say, this isn't your line of magic. It's not mine, either. But unless we can produce your simulacrum, you don't stand a chance in court. Not unless you want to plead insanity, and I think the D.A. would give us a hard time on that one. It's too close to election time, and this case is getting a lot of publicity."

"Now neither of us knows much about the Dark World, but my friend Jack has never been bothered much by legal niceties, nor has his education been limited. He may be a gypsy and an unlicensed warlock, but he knows more of the Art than any man or woman that I've ever been acquainted with."

"I resent having to consort with some half literate witch doctor, Njalsson, but I've trusted you this far. I guess I don't have much to lose," Fredericks said unhappily.

"You're right," Egil said, "only your life. But I want you to be careful with Jack and try not to offend him. He's a strange old bird, and he won't do a damn thing for you unless he wants to."

To his surprise, Jack greeted them at the shop's door, an anxious look on his face. Ignoring Fredericks, the old man asked Egil, "Are you all right then, lad. You had me worried. I caught the demon scent earlier when I read the cards concerning your fortune."

Fredericks snorted, causing Jack to give him the evil eye. To head off an incident, Egil related the details of his meeting with the demon.   Both men listened with professional interest.

"They would dare such a thing in broad daylight?" Fredericks interjected.

"Why not?" Egil asked, a little put out at his client. "As far as anyone could tell, he was a perfectly respectable businessman.   The Dark Powers are too clever to send a cloven hoofed monster after me. I wouldn't have been able to tell myself except for the absence of a reflection."

"It matters not, the meeting is over and you survived," Jack said. "But you were in danger, still are. I should have given you some protection when you left here. You must forgive an old and besotted gypsy. My memory isn't what it used to be."

"When have you forgotten anything, Jack?" Egil asked. "But they are getting nervous. Next time they might try something more drastic. If we are going to act, I think it best that we do so quickly."

"Yes," Jack agreed, "but not so quickly that we forget things in our haste. I sense that your client doubts me. Not that I am offended. We gypsies are used to non-believers. It was centuries before your science recognized the existence of the Art. Now they license it and hide it behind the name of technology. No, I am not offended. But tell me, Egil, will he grease the palm of a gypsy?"

"I think that I can guarantee that he will pay anything reasonable. I can draw up a contract that will be binding."

"You're a good lad, Egil.   Now as to the terms, five thousand dollars and your client goes free."

"Five thousand dollars. Njalsson, are you out of your mind?" Fredericks sputtered. "You don't actually expect me to pay this charlatan five thousand dollars?"

"Would you rather spend twenty years in prison or in an insane asylum, Fredericks?" Egil asked, starting to lose his patience with the man. "Judging from that apartment you were renting for Miss Friendly, I don't think that five thousand would be that much of a burden."

"This is no parlor trick that you are asking for, Mr. Fredericks," Jack said, emphasizing the name with a sneer. "You are asking me to deal with the Dark Powers. The risks are great — greater than you can imagine. 'The eternal torments of Hell' is not just an idle phrase. Five thousand dollars, take it or leave it."

"Look," Egil said, trying to conciliate the two men. "I don't think that there's much I can do without Jack's help. Unless we can produce the simulacrum, the evidence is against you. And I don't have the talents necessary to do that. Nor do I know anyone else who does. If Jack says that he can deliver, he can. If you aren't willing to trust me on that, then maybe you'd better find yourself another lawyer, because there isn't anything that I can do to help you."

Fredericks snorted, but agreed. "Very well, five thousand, but only on completion. And one more thing. I want Starenko. I want him implicated in this mess. He's caused me too much trouble."

"Don't press it. We're going to have enough trouble just proving that you're innocent." More haggling followed, but finally an agreement was reached and Egil drew up a contract with the two men affixing their signatures and Egil acting as witness.

With the business done, the gypsy escorted them back to a room Egil had never been in before. The walls were lined with books in at least a dozen languages, some of the volumes centuries old. The majority of the tomes were in Latin or Hebrew, though several were in Farsi or Arabic. At least one bore a title in Chinese ideograms. Those that the lawyer could read were treatises on Magic and the Art, but some, at least, were works he recognized only by reputation. To his surprise, there was almost a whole wall of modern works from the basic Feynman's Lectures on Metaphysics that he recalled from his freshman days to the more advance Knuth's series, Fundamental Spells and Seminumerical Rituals and the encyclopedic Bourbaki volumes on magical symbols and their algebraic manipulation.

It was a side of the old wizard that Egil had never suspected, the formal scholar.   Even Fredericks was impressed by the collection, and he looked at the old gypsy with new respect.   A major portion of the world's knowledge of the Art was represented by the books in that small room, and it put many university libraries to shame.

"I surprise even you, eh lad?" Old Jack asked Egil with a chuckle. "You thought that I was only a half crazy gypsy. Well maybe I am. But this is my private sanctum, my secret. Why don't I have it out front?   Some people are not impressed with your modern technology.   Their faith is in the old Art as it was practiced by my grandfather and by his. Too many books scare them. It's bad for business. Now quiet, while I consult."

It was not one of the volumes in Latin that he pulled down from the shelf, but a large tome bound in leather and bearing the marks of centuries of wear. The pages were of vellum and neither Egil nor Fredericks could recognize the handwritten script or the language. The gypsy was a long time pouring over the pages, occasionally making notes in a fine, neat, hand. The notes were written in English.

"Egil, you have told me that it is necessary to produce the simulacrum in order to prove that Mr. Fredericks is innocent," Jack said when he had finally closed the book. "Is it needful that this be done in court?"

"Well, that would be the best proof," the lawyer replied, "but it would probably be sufficient to produce it in front of witnesses, especially if they were from the police or the D.A.'s office. We could then at least raise the issue of reasonable doubt, and if the evidence is strong enough, we might even get the prosecutor to drop the case. But that would depend on how convincing it is."

"Good. I am glad that there is no need to conjure the demon in court. I do not think that I could do so. The particular type of demon we deal with is not easily bound or even summoned. Only where the influences are particularly strong, and the lure great do we have much hope of success." After a pause he added, "And survival."

"The best, perhaps the only place, would be the scene of the crime itself. There the demon is in part bound by its own past actions, and we have some hope of controlling it and making it answer for its crimes. But that is not sufficient to bring the demon through from the Dark World."

Jack turned to Fredericks and stared him in the eye. "Are you prepared to go through with this, Mr. Fredericks? Some men might think it better to go to prison than to risk what may happen. Your own safety is particularly at hazard, even more so than Egil's or my own. It is you that will act as the magnet to draw the demon to the summoning. And as the demon is bound to you, so are you bound to the demon."

"I am willing. I'm, not one of those men who would rather have the safety of a prison," Fredericks said stiffly.

"Good. You will need your bravery before this is through." He seemed to consider the matter settled for he turned to Egil and asked, "You, Egil, will arrange for the witnesses from the police? You know of such men that you can trust?"

"Yeah, at least I think so. Joe O'Neil is pretty honest, and he should know of at least one other cop. If there is one. I also have a friend in the D.A.'s office."

"Good, then I will leave that to you. Also, this Starenko that Mr. Fredericks is so keen on having revenge on — I think that he should be at the summoning. Can this be arranged?"

"I think I can persuade him. I can tell him that I want to sell Fredericks out, but for more than his demon offered me this afternoon. I can use the address book of Miss Friendly's as bait."

"Ah, the mind of the lawyer. Almost as devious as a gypsy. Now you, Mr. Fredericks. We will require certain items to effect the summoning. You understand that this is a particularly difficult conjuration and that the ingredients are far from ordinary. I believe that your firm is well supplied in these matters. Can you fill this shopping list by tomorrow evening?"

The scientist took the list, and while he was puzzled, he nodded affirmation. "I think that we have most of these. What we don't have I can get from our suppliers."

"Good," Old Jack said. "Remember, only the best quality. Your life may depend on it."

"There remains one detail. The two detectives you told me about. The shape strong one and the other that tracked Mr. Fredericks to your office. I think that they are involved in this matter, too, and should be present at its resolution. You, with Mr. Fredericks and myself, form a three. The witnesses you mentioned form a second.   The two detectives with Starenko would form a third three. Three threes for nine. It would make for a pleasant symmetry. And it would make it easier to balance the Powers. Nine was a number of great significance to your ancestors, Egil.

Nine worlds under Yggdrasil. Nine Norns. Nine times nine sacrifices every nine years at Uppsala. It's too tempting."

"Unfortunately we have nothing to serve as bait, and I am not sure that they would come if we invited them," Egil replied.

"They didn't, by any chance, leave anything personal in your office during their visit?"

"Not that I remember. They didn't exactly linger," Egil said as he stuffed his hands in his pockets. Doing so, he felt a wad of greasy paper. "Wait a minute. They didn't leave anything behind, but I did write down their names and badge numbers. Would that be any help?" He produced the hamburger wrapping with the names and numbers.

"It could be better, but we have no time to be choosy. The names are too public to retain much power, but the numbers. A number is sometimes better than a name. It is in part secret and therefore more powerful in the naming."

Egil saw what the sorcerer was getting at. It is a basic tenet of magic that the symbol is the object. "I think that I can insure that they will be there. We will meet tomorrow, and I will instruct you in the part each must play. But now I think that we should get our rest. We will need our strength tomorrow night."

☆　☆　☆　☆　☆

It took all of Njalsson's skill at persuasion to convince his friend on the D.A.'s staff to permit them to use the apartment. It was "extremely irregular", as the assistant prosecutor had put it. It had been even harder to get him to agree to act on his own authority without informing the D.A. The prosecutor was basing his hopes in the upcoming election on a successful conviction in the Friendly case. He was not likely to favor investigations that could complicate matters.

O'Neil proved easier. He was a good cop and well aware of the corruption in the department. If he could do anything to help clean it up he was only too willing to help. Also, irregularities bothered the pragmatic policeman less that the assistant prosecutor.

Midnight, the approximate hour of the crime, had been chosen for the summoning, both for that reason and for the symbolic importance of the dividing line between one day and the next. The conspirators arrived several hours early to make the final preparations. Despite Jack's admonition, none of them had gotten much sleep. There had been too many things to arrange and too little time in which to do them. Fredericks showed the effects by a red eyed nervousness even more pronounced than his normal state. Egil responded by yawning. Only Old Jack seemed unaffected.

The crime lab people had long since finished in the apartment and sealed it, leaving them free from disturbances. The broken furniture had been cleaned up, but the thick, white carpet still bore the stains of the victim's blood. Fredericks had blanched when he had first seen it, and afterwards he took exaggerated care to avoid stepping on the discolored patches. Egil felt sorry for the little man in a way. He had really loved the woman, which was perhaps more than she had deserved. She had tried to steal his most valued possession. But then, love is blind.

Jack went to work with little hesitation. A low coffee table was converted into an altar by the addition of a covering of black velvet. On this altar he laid out the book and a silver arthame or magical knife. Other materials for the ritual were then laid out.

"This is costing me a fortune," Fredericks muttered to Egil. "Your old wizard has chosen some of the rarest substances known to science."

"So? Maybe you life is not worth the best?" Old Jack asked before returning to his preparation of a mixture of sulfur, frankincense, and myrrh. "This is not some gentle wood sprite that we summon. It takes strong bonds to hold a demon of the Dark World."

Without waiting for an answer, he lit the incense which filled the room with a cloying, thick scent. The sulfur didn't help matters, nor did the fact that Jack insisted that the windows remain shut.

Next, a vessel was produced, and into it the blood of a sanctified goat was poured. The use of sacrificial blood was frowned on by the scientific community, partly due to the pressures of antivivisectionists, but few denied its primal power. With a whisk of hair from a human virgin who had died of suicide, Old Jack applied blood to the stains on the carpet so that their surfaces were once again wet and shiny as they had been on the night of the murder. As much as possible, they had recreated the apartment as it had been that night. Even the weather had cooperated by providing another cold, damp rain.

One more step needed completion. Using a mixture of lead, quicksilver, silver, and gold, the gypsy began to paint a pentagram on the carpet. Three circles he drew, the outer one almost as large across as his arms could stretch, the centermost no more than a cubit in diameter. A nine and a six pointed star enclosed the second and third rings respectively with a triangle inscribing the innermost. Irreverently, Egil thought that it was a good thing the carpet had already been ruined by bloodstains; otherwise the landlord would not be very happy with the mess they were making.

Jack had taken great care not to close any of the circles, but had left a break as wide as a hand in each. Using the queer script of the ancient grimoire, he wrote an invocation within each and then closed the circle with an elaborate flourish. The openings were spaced 120 degrees apart from each other, and the gypsy backed out of the circles as if they were a maze taking care not to cross any of the lines. It was essential to maintain the fiction that the pentagram was a physical barrier. By the symbolism of magic it would become one for the demon they would conjure.

"My preparations are finished. Please do not disturb them." Jack said. "Officer O'Neil, have you the silver bullets?"

"Sure. But it seems a waste of good metal. Lead will stop a man better."

"Remember, one of those here tonight will be a werewolf. If it should become necessary, use the silver bullets and no other. Lead will have no effect on him." The Irishman nodded though it was clear that he had little knowledge of the subtleties of magic. "Egil, have you the blade of cold iron as I asked you? I hope such is not needed, but as a last resort demons have a dread of that metal."

The lawyer brought out the hunting knife that he had borrowed from a neighbor. It was little enough of a weapon against the Dark Powers, but its well balanced weight felt comfortable in his hand. Old Jack examined it and then nodded with satisfaction. "I think it best if each now takes his place. All except Egil should be out of sight."

The policemen and the prosecutor retired to the bedroom where they would be out of sight but able to hear what was going on. After they had gone, Jack set up two small dolls on the altar. One had a tiny badge with a number inscribed on it; the other had a pointed set of ears like a werewolf. Egil had thought it best if he not inform his friend in the prosecutor's office that they were attempting to involve a pair of detectives as well as Starenko and the demon.   He noted with satisfaction that a tiny bit of wolfbane had been tied around the werewolf doll's neck.

There was nothing to do but wait.   The lawyer's earlier fatigue had given way to tension as the preparations had progressed.   Now he gazed nervously out at the rain through the glass of the apartment's sliding doors.

"You are worried, Egil?" Jack asked.   He nodded with approval.   "Good.   Then you will be careful.   What we attempt tonight is serious business."

"It's a little out of my league," Egil said, relaxing just a bit.   "It's not the sort of thing I used to do when I was a student at CalThaum."

"It should not be in anybody's league.   Sometimes I think that the world would have been better if the scientists had never discovered the Art and the validity of the principles of magic.   At best they waste it on tricks like that swimming pool out there."   The old man nodded at the pool which they could see out past the railing of the balcony.   Despite the rain it was still surrounded by a dome of warm, dry air, the magically transposed climate of southern California.

"That's a good piece of commercial magic.   It's cheaper than heating the pool or building it inside," Egil said defensively.

"That's the problem.   The Art has been bent to profit. That is what this Starenko would do despite the consequences.   It would be better if magic had been left to a handful of crazy old gypsies."

They had no further time to continue the discussion.   A knock sounded at the door.

"Come in," Egil said, trying to keep his voice steady.   The door opened slowly, and in the flickering shadows of the candle flames he could make out the form of Starenko, the face dark and sinister in the wavering light.

"What's this all about, Njalsson? What is this mumbo jumbo you've got here? When you called you said that you had some information that you wanted to sell me."

"It's a book, Mr. Starenko," Egil said holding up the address book of Diane Friendly. He wanted to keep Starenko busy while Jack completed his spell. He also wanted him to incriminate himself if possible.

"It belonged to the murdered girl, and it contains your address. The D.A. might find it interesting reading. But then again, we might arrange terms so that he never saw it."

"Why should I care if he saw it? My name isn't the only one in that book, and the D.A. has got an open and shut case against Fredericks."

"If he could link you to industrial espionage as well as to the girl, he might want to take a closer look at the case. After all, we both know that it wasn't Fredericks that killed the girl. If the D.A. worked at it, he might even be able to prove it."

"All right, Njalsson," Starenko spat. "How much do you want to keep quiet and give me the book? Will you take ten thousand?"

"Ten thousand, Starenko? What you are asking for is a serious breach of my professional ethics. Besides, we both might find it convenient if I were free to travel. Let's say, oh, a hundred and fifty thousand. With that much I could stay away a nice long time. Perhaps even spend several years in Europe. Now wouldn't that suit your purposes?"

Egil hoped that he had gotten Starenko so say enough to convince the prosecutor. He didn't know how much longer he could hold Starenko's attention.

"I could have you put away for much less than that. Permanently. Twenty five thousand is my last offer. Don't push your luck."

"You can't afford to put me away. Two murders might look suspicious. It might start people wondering. I don't think that your employers at American Alchemical would appreciate any scandal."

That seemed to sober Starenko up. He mulled over his position silently for a moment. The two detectives chose that point to make their entrance. The werewolf was agitated, and his face looked as though he were breaking out in hives. The other took in the scene and then recognizing Starenko asked, "Mr. Starenko, what gives? What are you doing here with the shyster? We didn't think anybody would be here, but my partner had this notion that we should check the place out. It was almost an obsession."

Neither one of the detectives seemed clear as to why they were there.

"Just what game are you playing at, Njalsson?" Starenko asked suspiciously. "What are these two bumblers doing here?"

"I thought that if I was going to make a deal all the parties involved should be here," Egil answered. "There's another one that should be here, but fortunately, he's just in the next room."

Fredericks took his cue to appear. For a moment Starenko stared in horror at the small scientist as if he represented a great danger. He was too intent on Fredericks to notice Old Jack quietly reciting from the book on the altar.

Starenko seemed to have guessed the true identity of the man he faced. Taking courage he said, "I can see what you're trying to do now, Njalsson. It won't do you any good. Neither one of you is going to leave this room alive."

A small automatic pistol had appeared in his hand, its barrel pointed half way between Egil and Fredericks. Behind the altar Jack kept up his almost inaudible droning.

"I don't think you'll use that gun, Starenko," Egil said with more confidence than he felt. "Our little party isn't quite complete, but we have only a few moments to wait." An antique clock on the mantle began to chime the strokes of midnight.

In front of the altar the center of the pentagram began to glow with a baleful light of its own, and the smell of sulfur, strong already from the incense was now almost overpowering. All of them, including the two cops and the assistant D.A. who had come out of the bedroom turned towards the circle. Starenko's gun lowered as a duplicate of Fredericks wavered and then solidified.

The resemblance amazed Egil. He could hardly tell the two apart except for one difference. The one in the pentagram had unusual eyes. He had seen that cold, cruel stare once before him in a man sitting next to him in his own automobile.

"You fools. Do you know what you've done?" Starenko shouted, his voice almost a scream.

"What have you done, Mr. Starenko?" the D.A.'s man asked. "It appears that we have two Fredericks here, which would throw some doubt on which one committed the murder. Perhaps you could enlighten us on that subject, Mr. Starenko. You had some interesting things to say earlier."

Starenko looked like a cornered rat. He could see the polished barrels of the two police .38's wielded by O'Neil and his friend. A quick glance told him that he could expect no help from the were-detective or his partner. Slowly he began to back towards the fireplace.

"I'll get you for this, Njalsson," Starenko shouted. Looking towards the demon in the circle he spoke the words, "Elat padrash gorvon." The demon tried to press forward through the walls of the pentagram, but was met by an invisible barrier. Egil swore that he heard a hiss come from the demon. Before his eyes the features that had been Fredericks began to waver as the demon changed shape, metamorphisizing into the cool killer that had threatened the lawyer in his car.

"Your demon won't help you this time. We have him contained." With the demon safely trapped, Egil felt his confidence returning. Slowly he advanced towards Starenko.

"If I'm going down, we're all going down," Starenko cried. Grabbing a poker from the fireplace he approached the three circles. The tool was wrought iron, and as the lawyer grasped the other's intentions it was his turn to panic. With slow purposeful strokes the criminal broke each of the three rings in turn.

With the last ring broken the demon began to swell, growing into a scaled horror that nearly touched the ceiling. Sulfur was steaming on the skin of the beast as if it were hot to the touch. The horns and cloven hooves were visible. As Egil watched, a tongue of flame licked out from the demon to envelope Starenko. A moment later all that remained of the man was a tiny pile of glowing cinders.

The two detectives made a dash for the door, but it did little to save them. They were caught as they crossed the threshold, leaving the jambs of the doorway charred and smoking. Ignoring the others the demon spun and jumped through the glass doors and out over the balcony railing.

Egil grabbed Jack's arm and asked frantically, "What's happening?"

"Starenko forgot that it was I and not he who had conjured the demon this time. He no longer had control of it. The demon, as demons will, hated him for the power that Starenko had exercised over him. Freed from any bonds he did what came naturally. He killed the one he hated most."

"Enough of explanations," Jack said impatiently. "The demon is loose without any restraints. If something is not done quickly he will kill again and again. More importantly, the demon can serve as a bridgehead for the forces of the Dark World to enter this world."

"What can we do?" Egil asked grimly.

"I no longer have any power over the demon. He must be defeated with cold steel. It's up to you. I only hope that your heart is as good as that of your Viking ancestors."

O'Neil had been listening. He grabbed up the poker and set off down the hall. Egil realized that he could do no less. He followed on the Irishman's heels, the hunting knife drawn and ready in his hand. It seemed a puny weapon for that which he faced.

At least a dozen people were out on the lawn when they reached the ground floor, but they didn't need them to find the demon. A trail of burning shrubbery tracked it across the yard to where the demon stood. The beast seemed puzzled and confused, and it turned as if it were looking for something. In the distance sounded the wail of a fire engine.

Egil was reluctant to close in on the demon. Its fiery breath could shoot out at least twenty feet, and he had seen what it had done to Starenko. He moved cautiously, circling in front of the demon. The cold eyes seemed to follow the tip of the knife Egil held.

While Egil held its attention, O'Neil had moved behind the beast, the poker held aloft in his hands like a club.

Suddenly he darted forward bringing all the weight of his two hundred pounds down with the poker. Roaring the demon spun and bounced the cop to one side before returning to advance on Egil.

Egil stepped back, his eyes fastened on the demon. Out of the corner of his vision he could see Jack and Fredericks on the grass with the other horrified onlookers.

"Egil, lad," Jack cried out. "The pool, the pool. The spell on the pool might weaken the demon's power. Try to lure him within the circle."

Egil glanced behind himself, almost tripping in the process. Behind and to his left the circle of dry grass lay only thirty feet away. Twenty feet beyond that was the blue lit water of the pool. He changed his direction so that he was backing straight for the water.

He had almost made it — almost crossed the dividing line of the spell when the demon pounced. Egil held the knife out hoping the demon would impale itself on the point, but a blow from the huge paw spun him around and knocked the knife away onto the grass. For a moment he was dazed, then looking up he saw the demon towering above him. He tried to scuttle away into the safety of the pool side circle.

It didn't look as though he'd reach it, but a cry from the crowd checked the demon's advance. "You killed her! You killed her!"

Egil could recognize the voice as belonging to Fredericks. The demon had turned to face away from the lawyer to watch the scientist. To his surprise, the little man was advancing on the demon a look of hatred and madness on his face. As he watched, his client scooped up the knife from where it had fallen and turned it towards the beast.

There was almost a look of fear on the demon's face, and its body began to shrink and change shape until once again it was the image of Fredericks. The demon moved back, crossing over the spell line surrounding the pool. Fredericks followed, and then just as the demon reached the lip of the pool he ran forward with the knife.

The blade sank into the demon's breast, and as man and demon met they plunged into the water. There was a hissing of steam and a great fountain of water spraying high in the air. When the steam had cleared, Egil could see that the water level had been lowered by several feet.

The lawyer staggered upright and approached the pool. There was nothing to be seen of the demon. Fredericks was there floating on the surface face down, his neck bent at an unnatural angle. There was no doubt that he was dead.

Egil remained staring at the corpse until Jack came to take his arm and pull him away. "It's done, lad, and nothing can change the way it came out."

He let himself be set down on one of the brightly colored chairs surrounding the pool. Across from him a fireman was bandaging O'Neil's arm and putting it in a sling.

"He's dead then, is he?" the cop asked, seeing the answer written on Egil's face. "He was a brave one there at the end."

"He actually loved her."

"Loved who?" the cop asked in puzzlement.

"Diane Friendly, the murdered girl," Egil answered. "That's why he went after the demon, because it had killed her. Even after she had betrayed him, he still loved her enough to go to his death."

"I'm not sure that he had much choice," Jack said, for once looking tired and drawn.

"I was afraid that this might happen, but there was nothing I could do to guard against it. Once the demon had been conjured in his image, their fates were bound together. Fredericks wanted revenge too badly to allow them to separate. It's lucky for you that he did, though. I thought you were going to die on me, lad."

"I didn't die, but I managed to mess things up pretty well. My client is dead along with my chance to make much of a fee," the lawyer said, finally pulling himself together. "And I have a feeling that I'm going to have a lot of explaining to do over tonight."

"Don't think badly of yourself," Jack said. "You did as well as any man could. You've proved that Fredericks was innocent, and the guilty have been punished. Nor will this night go unnoticed. You've showed your skill. There will be others in need."

"Yeah, sure. That's what I keep telling myself."

DO VAMPIRES NOT BLEED?

DO VAMPIRES NOT BLEED?

☆   ☆   ☆   ☆   ☆

I was working late. This wasn't unusual for me. Business was better than when I had started the practice a few years earlier, but I still wasn't making enough to hire a secretary or paralegal. Besides, I liked the quiet that night brought. It made it easier to concentrate while working. It seemed that many of my clients preferred the night as well. Guess that says something about my clients.

When I looked up while reaching for a reference book, I noticed him sitting in the chair across from my desk. I hadn't heard him come in. He was of medium build, dark hair, swarthy complexion. He was dressed impeccably, custom tailoring — quality but not showy. My nostrils flared. I didn't need to see his lack of reflection to know he was a vampire.

I'd run into a few vampires before, but not many. For obvious reasons they are not usually welcomed in polite society, or most other societies for that matter. The tolerance of our modern age only goes so far. More than most "others", they are feared and shunned. But vampires are an ancient race and they have their own sources of power. As long as they kept their activities from intruding on the public eye they survived.

"Do not fear, Mr. Njalsson," the vampire said in an oily voice. "I am here as a client." He had a vaguely foreign accent, but one that I couldn't quite place

This took me by surprise. I suppose that my client base tends to be a bit unorthodox by the standards of most lawyers, but I'd never been retained before by one of the undead. The fact that I had earned a degree from the California Institute of Thaumaturgy before going into the law gave me a background in the arcane that most lawyers didn't have. That and word of mouth had brought some interesting cases my way. Not necessarily high paying, but interesting.

"What exactly can I do for you, Mr. — ?"

"Tolkas, Zoltan Tolkas. It's a legal matter. A rather simple one. Someone is trying to evict me from my place of residence. As you can understand, I would find that most inconvenient."

Inconvenient indeed, if he was referring to the place where he spent the daylight hours. The old legend about a vampire having to spend the daylight hours in some of his native soil was just that, a legend. However they did form an attachment to their place of rest and drew power from it. Being displaced would weaken him considerably as well as remove him from whatever defensive measures he had put in place over the years, thus leaving him vulnerable to his enemies.

"Well, Mr. Tolkas, I'm not sure I can help you. My practice is mostly criminal law, not property matters."

I left unsaid that the legal status of vampires was at best an open question. As "undead" rather than being among the living, it wasn't clear vampires had any legal standing in court. My experience with the case law on the subject was limited, but I knew that vampires did not have the same rights as, say, werewolves. I also knew that it was an area with few precedents. Vampires tended to stay out of courts.

"You do yourself an injustice, Mr. Njalsson. I have followed your career with interest. You have shown yourself both resourceful and diligent in protecting your clients interests. There are certain aspects of this matter which you are uniquely equipped to handle."

I was intrigued, but still reluctant to take the case. I'd never been fond of vampires.

"I still don't see how I can help you. I have a number of other cases on my plate right now."

"Is it that you don't want to help me, Mr. Njalsson? Because I am a vampire? An Undead? A hideous monster undeserving of consideration? I have money. I can pay your fee. Don't I deserve justice? That's all I'm asking, Mr. Njalsson. Justice."

Ah, ethics, they will get you into trouble every time. "You should have been a lawyer yourself, Mr. Tolkas. Alright. I'll look into your matter. If you have a case to make, I'll charge you my standard rates. If I don't think there is anything I can do, I won't charge you."

"I expected nothing less from you, Mr. Njalsson. You have my thanks. I have a file of the relevant papers here. Also, one thousand dollars as a retainer to show I am in earnest. If, as you say, there is nothing you can do, you can refund what you think appropriate. And, now, I will take my leave and take up no more of your time. Thank you, Mr. Njalsson."

He stood with a flourish and left by the office door. I was almost disappointed. I had half expected him to disappear in a puff of smoke or turn himself into a bat. Of course, as I listened I couldn't hear his footsteps in the hall or hear the elevator.

I looked over the documents he had given me. They were for a house in one of the older sections of town. The houses tended to be big and solid, but not mansions. A lot of them had been converted to apartments over the years. It wasn't a trendy neighborhood, but not an address to be ashamed of either. There was a deed and a transfer of title dated seventy five years earlier, a copy of the latest property tax bill and a receipt. All were in the name of Zoltan Tolkas. All looked legitimate. As far as I could see, Mr. Tolkas paid his bills on time.

The problem was that condemnation proceedings had been initiated on the grounds that the property had been abandoned as there was no living owner. The file included a newspaper clipping saying that a company called the "South Side Development Corporation" was planning to put up a large apartment building on the block and had bought up most of the other properties in question. Tolkas was one of two holdouts at this point, the other being an eighty-five year old woman named Gladys Smith. There was nothing to indicate that she was a vampire. The city seemed to backing the condemnation as part of a larger "redevelopment" scheme. In this town that usually meant the mayor and some aldermen were getting kickbacks.

On the surface it all seemed too normal. Despite what my client seemed to think, there didn't seem to be any supernatural elements involved. Just money and politics. I thought to myself that it might be interesting to take a case that didn't involve dark powers. It did look like I'd have to do some research and find out just who the South Side Development Corporation was and who they were paying off.

☆   ☆   ☆   ☆   ☆

I spent the next morning at the court house checking property records. The prices South Side had paid for the other houses on the block had been above market rate. Not outrageously so, but enough to show that South Side really wanted the block. I tried to track down South Side too, but that proved a lot harder. South Side Development, it turned out, was owned by Urban Interests which in turn was a subsidiary of Newco Limited. Newco itself was somewhat shadowy and as they were registered out of state I'd have to use other sources to find out who they really were.

I put in a call to a friend that worked on the paper to see what he knew — which was nothing — but he said that he'd check around and get back to me. He asked me if I thought there was a story in it, and I said I didn't know yet.

After grabbing a quick lunch at a tavern across from the court house that served a mean burger and one of the better local beers on tap, I decided to check out the property in question.

It was about what I had expected; a solid brick house of the kind known as a four-square, probably built around the turn of the last century. It was big, solid, had two stories and wide eaves but nothing much to distinguish it from any number of other houses in the neighborhood. I did have to say that Tolkas kept it up. It was certainly no eyesore. The paint on the trim was in good shape. Even the lawn was kept up nicely. I wondered if Tolkas did his gardening in the moonlight or if he had someone do it for him. Most of the houses on the block were in good shape, though several had been boarded up recently. It seemed a shame to tear them down in the name of progress.

As long as I was in the neighborhood I thought I'd drop in on the only other person who hadn't sold out — Ms. Gladys Smith. Her place was two doors down from Tolkas'. It was a Queen Anne that could use a coat of paint, but other than that wasn't in bad shape. As I walked up to the front steps I could see a pair of eyes peaking out behind some lace curtains. Ms. Smith seemed to be at home.

I rang the bell, but there was no answer. I knocked on the door, then a little louder. She must have figured I wasn't going to go away, so she finally answered the door.

"If you're from South Side, I haven't changed my mind," she said as she poked her head out the door narrowly cracked door. Gladys Smith was your typical old lady — thin, about five foot two, wearing old lady clothes. She looked like you could knock her over with a feather. But she'd probably jump right back up and dare you to do it again.

"I'm not from South Side, Mrs. Smith," I said. "My name is Njalsson, and I'm a lawyer. I've been hired by your neighbor, Mr. Tolkas. Would you mind if I ask you a few questions?"

"It's Miss Smith, Mr. Njalsson. I don't usually talk to strangers, but seeing as you know Mr. Tolkas, I suppose it is alright." She opened the door a little wider and invited me in.

It didn't look like the place had changed in half a century. Everything was neat and tidy, but nothing was newer than the forties. Most of the furniture looked as if it was older than that.

"You get along with Mr. Tolkas, then?" I asked.

"Oh, not socially, you understand. You know he's foreign. But he seems like a nice man. Always dresses so well and keeps his yard nice. Why do you ask?"

"Oh, well, he just hired me yesterday and I don't know too much about him. Just curiosity. Have you lived in this house long?"

"All my life. I was born right here in the upstairs bedroom. It was my parents until they passed away. I just never wanted to move. I still don't want to, no matter how much they want to pay me. I just wouldn't want to move into one of those old folks homes. It just wouldn't feel right."

"I can understand that, Miss Smith. My client feels the same way. He's lived in his place quite a while, I believe."

"Oh, goodness, yes," she exclaimed putting her hand to her mouth. "He bought his place when I was a little girl. I must have been ten or so. Kept to himself, though. Never came out during the day. I think he has one of those night time jobs."

I wondered what one of those "night time jobs" might be in Miss Smith's mind. Maybe a night watchman? Actually, not a bad job for a vampire. It made me wonder where my client got his money.

"Gee, that would make him over ninety years old. He seems to be in pretty good shape."

"Now that you mention it, Mr. Njalsson, he never seems to age. He looks today just like he did when I was a little girl. How strange. Oh, but that couldn't be. It must just be a young girl's imagination. You know when you're young all the grownups look so old."

It was clear that she hadn't a clue that Tolkas was a vampire. I decided to get back to the business at hand. "You say that South Side has been trying to get you to sell?"

"Oh, yes. They keep bothering me about it. They were nice at first. Offered me a lot of money, and kept saying how nice the retirement communities — that's what they called them, retirement communities — how nice they were, activities and trips and such. Offered to take me to visit one. But of course I didn't go. I don't need any activities. I've got plenty to keep me busy here. And I just don't see any reason to leave."

"Anyway, after a while they started getting downright nasty. Talked about condemning my house and eminent domain and I don't know all what. Said I'd better take their offer now, and if I waited, I might not get as much money. As if that mattered. My parents left me a trust that is more than adequate enough. That's why I didn't come to the door. I thought you were them." She said them as if it were a swear word, not that Miss Smith would ever swear.

"Well, thank you for your time, Miss Smith," I finally said. I didn't think that I'd learn much more. "Mr. Tolkas doesn't want to sell, either. Maybe I can get South Side to change their plans."

"Oh, that would be wonderful, Mr. Njalsson!" she gushed. "They are getting to be such a bother."

I didn't have that much hope, myself, but it didn't seem right that a nice little old lady should have to move. Or a nice, little old vampire, either. Yeah right. I said goodbye and watched as Gladys Smith latched the door behind me. She waved and I waved back.

☆   ☆   ☆   ☆   ☆

The visit had been interesting if not necessarily useful. I was beginning to wonder how a vampire could live out in the open for seventy five years without attracting any attention or suspicion. Maybe I knew less about vampires than I thought. There was one place I knew where I could get more information.

Jack ran what ostensibly was an antique store. Not that I had ever seen anyone buy anything there. His customers tended to come for different reasons. Jack was a hedge wizard. He had no formal training in the art, at least none that would allow him to get a license. Which is how I had met him in the first place, defending him in a case of practicing magic without a license. It had been my first case, and I had lost. But Jack had appreciated my efforts, anyway, and the fact that I paid his fine out of my own pocket.

Most of his business was small time stuff; telling fortunes, reading palms, casting the tarot cards. That or making love potions, protection spells. His prices were reasonable and most of his stuff actually worked. Jack was the real deal. He didn't have any fancy degree on his wall, but he knew more about the Art than most of the professors at CalThaum. I don't know where he had learned it; in fact I didn't know anything about him for certain. It wasn't that he was secretive with me. It was that he never told the same story twice. I've heard him claim to be a gypsy, an Indian brujo, a kabalist, a follower of an obscure 13th Century Tibetan monk. He even claimed to be Leprechaun once, but that was on St. Padraig's day and I chalked it up to the bottle of Jamison's we were sharing. His stories were always detailed and the facts that I could investigate checked out. He even had proof. Hanging on the walls of his inner sanctum were old pictures of gypsies, Indians, students at a Yeshiva — you name it. In each one there was a man that could be Jack looking not a day younger than he did now, though some of them looked to have been taken over a hundred years ago. I'd long ago given up trying to sort out what to believe and what not to.

The one thing I was certain of was that he knew his lore. He could read at least twenty languages including some which were no longer spoken. He had a library that would have put most universities metaphysics section to shame. Grimoires, Kabala, spellbooks, even mathematics and quantum mechanics. There were some volumes that I'd seen that my professors in college had insisted didn't even exist. And Jack hadn't just read them, he knew them by heart.

Most importantly, Jack had a knowledge of those areas of magic that are forbidden. Not that he practiced the black arts. He was a white wizard plain and simple. But if you needed to know what your enemy was up to, Jack was your man.

"Egil, my boy," he greeted me as I entered his shop, "It's been a while since you've come to see me."

"Things have been quiet."

"Ah, but that has changed, hasn't it?" he asked with a gleam in his eye.

"I'm not sure. I've got a case where I've realized that I don't know as much as maybe I should. I thought you might lend me the benefit of your experience over a drink or two." I waved the brown paper bag containing a bottle that I'd brought as an offering.

"Beware of lawyers bearing gifts." he joked. "Let's retire to my office."

His office was a small room in the back of the shop. It's where he kept his books and supplies. As far as I knew, I was the only one he ever invited back there.

He took the bag, read the label on the bottle, and nodded approvingly. "Scotch. Business must be good."

He brought down a couple of glasses from a shelf and a bottle of water from a small refrigerator. He opened the seal on the bottle and poured a couple of fingers of the brown liquid into each glass, adding just a splash of water. We moved over to his work table and sat down. We each took a sip and sat in silence for a few moments. He was waiting for me to start.

"What do you know about vampires?" I finally asked.

"What's to know? They're dead but not dead. They drink blood. One of your clients have vampire problems?"

"One of my clients is a vampire."

"You're sure? He's not just one of those poor fools that pretends to be one?"

"I know enough to know a vampire when I see one. He doesn't deny it either."

"Unusual. Vampires aren't usually big on the law."

"Well someone's trying to evict him. He wants me to stop them."

"Not unreasonable, I suppose. Though I would think a true vampire would have better methods to protect his interests. No offense."

"Well he doesn't seem to fit the normal image of a vampire," I explained. I went on to recount what I knew, including the situation of Miss Gladys Smith. Jack has a soft spot for underdogs. He might not be eager to help out a vampire, but an old lady in distress? He'd drop everything in a minute.

"Unusual, but not unheard of," Jack replied when I had finished relating my story. "Not all vampires are as you see in the movies. Vampires are an ancient race, and the war between the living and the undead has gone on for millennia. The undead have powers, but their numbers are small making it easy for the living to hunt them down. Some have found it safer to live in obscurity than to flaunt the trappings of power."

"But how do they survive? Don't they have to feed on blood?"

"Yes, but they don't have to kill — at least not often. The blood of a pig or other animal will sustain them. Your Mr. Tolkas may not have tasted human blood for years — even decades."

That made me feel a little better. My client might not pose a threat to humanity or his neighbor, Gladys Smith.

"Okay. He doesn't go around sucking blood and leaving corpses. But how does he pay his taxes?"

"How should I know? That's for you to find out. Maybe he is a night watchman?"

Jack was right. There are plenty of jobs where the workers never need to see the light of day. Bartenders, night watchmen, factory workers on the graveyard shift. It was something that I would have to investigate.

"So my client, the vampire, is just minding his own business, working the late shift every day until some big corporation wants to condemn his house to put up apartments and by the way they want to save a few bucks by not paying him for his place."

"It's not impossible. You're the lawyer. It seems that this is much more up your alley than mine. Now if you don't mind, pass the bottle over here."

I obliged after pouring a couple more fingers of whisky in my glass. After that Jack spent the next several hours recounting various bits of vampire lore. Some of it was things that I knew already, but much of what he told me was details that they hadn't mentioned in college. The undead smacked of the black arts and had been glossed over in my classes. It was nearly eight when I left Jack with half a bottle of Irish whisky.

I was fumbling with the key to my apartment door when I was approached by someone I didn't recognize as being one of my neighbors. That was odd because the building had a security door on the entrance. It wasn't the greatest building; shabby in a genteel sort of way, but we didn't have much problem with crime or loiterers. The residents weren't rich enough to attract the attention of professional thieves and the building was respectable enough to keep out the riff raff.

He didn't look like either a thief or a bum. He was dressed in a suit, good but not too good. At first I thought he might be a salesman, but he wasn't carrying a sample case.

"Mr. Njalsson?" he asked, but it was plain that he knew the answer already because he continued without letting me answer. "I represent the South Side Development Corporation. Can we step into your apartment for a minute? There's a matter that I'd like to discuss with you."

"Look, it's late and I've had a few drinks. If it is brief, you can tell me here in the hallway. If not, see me in my office tomorrow."

"Very well. My employer is willing to make an offer for your client's property. It's a fair offer, above market rate. For reasons that you're well aware of, we don't have to make this offer, but in the interest of expediency we are doing so anyway. We think it would be best if you persuaded your client to accept." He pulled an envelope from his inside breast pocket and handed it to me.

"I'll look it over and pass it on to my client if it seems reasonable. You can tell your employer we will be in touch if he decides to accept. And now, if you'll excuse me, I'd like to go to bed."

He looked as if he were going to say something and then thought better of it. I opened my door, went through and shut it in his face. I pressed my ear against the wood and after a few moments I heard his footsteps receding down the hall. I took a piece of chalk that I keep near the door for just such occasions and marked a sequence of symbols around the frame of the door, not forgetting the floor in front of it. More than once I'd felt the need for more protection than a simple lock would provide. The spell wasn't powerful enough to keep out a really powerful wizard or demon, but it would work on the hired hands. I wasn't sure about the bit about vampires not being able to come in uninvited. I wasn't going to risk it. And it sure was interesting that South Sides representative had most definitely been a vampire.

☆   ☆   ☆   ☆   ☆

I was in my office the next afternoon when my friend at the paper called and asked if I wanted to meet him for a drink. He said he had some information for me. We set a time and place to meet and then he hung up without giving me any more information.

The bar he had chosen was across from the paper's offices. At night it was a popular sports bar, particularly if there was a game at the arena down the street, but before the sports crowd showed up it was frequented mostly by reporters. It was an old place with tin ceilings and a massive backbar of dark wood and mirrors. The beer was good and they made a pretty decent burger. I ordered a tap and waited at the bar till my friend came.

When he arrived he ordered a beer and a whiskey chaser, downed the shot and then motioned that we should go over to one of the tables off to the side.

"You look like you had a rough day," I said.

"Maybe you will feel like having a shot when I tell you what I found out."

"Did you find out who's behind South Side?"

"In a manner of speaking. Have you ever heard of a Vladimir Rascaski?"

"No. Is he involved with South Side?"

"Yes and no. South Side is part of a chain of front companies that is so complicated that it's hard to tell who owns what. The only time I've ever seen anything like it was when I was doing a story on mob involvement in business."

"So this Rascaski is in organized crime?" I asked.

"I didn't say that, though it wouldn't surprise me. It's just that no one goes to that much trouble unless they are trying to hide something."

"So what can you tell me about him?"

"Not much. He's a real man of mystery if you know what I mean. He keeps a real low profile. I couldn't find anything biographical about him — not in Who's Who, not in public records. As far as I can tell he's never even applied for a dog license."

"Maybe he just doesn't like dogs."

"Yeah, sure. Look, everybody leaves traces, and I'm real good at looking for them."

"So how do you know he's involved with South Side?"

"Oh, he's involved, alright. I didn't say that no one has heard of him. Everyone's heard of him. There just are no records. He likes to make a big splash. When South Side announced this apartment project he threw a big bash. All the city bigwigs were there. He was a real charmer, according to people I talked to. Had everyone eating out of his hand."

"The interesting thing is, there aren't any photos from the party. Normally when you throw a gala like that you invite all the media. You know, get your picture on the front page, footage on the ten o'clock news. Not Rascaski. No cameras allowed. Strictly enforced. I talked to one of our photographers that tried to cover the story. They had guys at all the doors — big bruiser types, checking everybody as they came in. Even had a diviner, you know, one of those guys who can sniff things out. They even stopped the wife of one of the guys on the city planning commission that had tried to bring a miniature camera in her purse. Wouldn't let her in unless she gave it up."

"What I figure is there's something crooked about this Rascaski guy and he doesn't want his picture getting around just in case someone should recognize him."

"Yeah, that could be," I said. Either that, or he knew that cameras couldn't take his picture and he didn't want that fact getting around. He didn't want people figuring out that he was a vampire.

"So just what have you got yourself into, buddy?" my friend asked. His interest was piqued, that was for sure. He could smell a story, he just didn't know what kind.

"I've got a client that has had his home condemned for this apartment project. He doesn't want to move. There's at least one other person that feels that way."

"I've got to tell you, this Rascaski has got the support of a lot of important people. Like the mayor and most of the aldermen. Also the owner of my paper. When I told my editor what I was doing he said to stop it. Said the paper doesn't want to cause trouble for a major developer that's just trying to improve the city. That's bull. I think the paper has been bought off. The paper and a lot of other people if you get what I mean. You could be getting yourself into a lot of trouble. Not that that would bother you."

"I'll keep that in mind. Thanks for the information. I've got to go now."

I was thinking that maybe I should have another talk with my client and see if there were things he had left out. I threw a ten on the table and said, "Have another one on me."

"Thanks. You let me know if anything big turns up. I don't care how much they've been bought off, if my editor sees a big enough story, he'll run it."

"You'll be the first to know," I said as I headed towards the door.

I figured that if I was going to talk to my client, my best bet would be to catch him at his house right after dusk. I didn't expect to meet him coming out of his front door carrying a lunch bucket and with a copy of the evening paper tucked underneath his arm.

"Do you have a minute, Mr. Tolkas?"

"Well I'm on my way to work, but there's probably a few minutes until my bus comes if you want to wait with me."

I followed him down to the corner bus stop. "Just what line of work are you in?"

"I work for the county. I'm the night clerk at the county morgue," he said almost apologetically. A perfect job for a vampire, I thought to myself. The hours were right and it was a good bet that Tolkas wouldn't be spooked spending his time with corpses.

"Have you been working there long?"

"Forty years now. I know some people might not think much of it, but it's a steady job. People are always going to be dying. I don't have to worry about getting laid off. And no one else wants the late shift."

"Sounds like you enjoy your work."

"Not particularly, but it's a living," he said with a shrug. "You said you wanted to talk to me. I assume it was about more than my employment?" As he said the latter more of the vampire menace had crept into his voice.

"Yeah. I do. Do you know a Rascaski? It turns out he's the power behind South Side Development."

"Rascaski? I should have suspected. Yes, I know Rascaski. Of old, from the old country. We were enemies back then. But I thought that I had put all that behind me."

"Enemies? I thought Rascaski was a vampire, too?"

"Yes, but not of — how shall I say it — the same, clan? No, lineage would be a better term. Rascaski's line was always the more aggressive, the more violent. And they never liked to share. Not potential prey, not territory. My line was content with staying in the shadows, not attracting attention. Rascaski was always more ..." he hesitated as if searching for the right word, "flamboyant."

"So you think this Rascaski might have it in for you?"

"Oh, yes. He would not want to share our fair city with one who does not recognize his right to rule."

"Is there anything else you've left out? It seems like there would be a simpler way to getting rid of you than having you evicted?"

"I assure you, that is part of his goal. To evict me. To weaken me, and then, when I am powerless, to swoop down for the kill. That would be his way. But you are right, there is more to it. The house I live in is a location of power. I believe that before the white man came to this land it was a special place to the Indians. I draw from that power. It is part of the reason that I can exist without having to kill. Rascaski would want access to that power, but not because he wants to live in peace. He must be stopped, and not just for my sake. And now if you'll excuse me, my bus is coming."

I watched him board the bus, lunch pail and newspaper in hand. I still didn't like him, but he didn't seem evil — not like Rascaski. I'd have to do what I could to keep his house. His and Gladys Smith's.

There was to be a hearing on the condemnation proceedings before the planning commission. I had arranged to represent Gladys Smith as well as Tolkas in the matter — pro bono of course. Not that that was unusual. Fortunately, the hearing was at night so both my clients were able to attend. Tolkas had taken time off from work and was looking like a very respectable undertaker. Gladys Smith sat, prim and proper, in the front row looking like a figure from another age — in other words, like everyone's memory of their grandmother. It couldn't hurt.

The representatives of South Side Development spoke first. As far as I could tell Rascaski wasn't in attendance. He probably figured it was a lock. The spokesman was a slick type by the name of Lawrence Wilson, in a five hundred dollar suit. He looked confident. After all, the commissioners were mostly on Rascaski's payroll and it was a minor meeting on a simple condemnation proceeding. What could go wrong?

What he didn't know was that I had gotten word out to all the urban preservationists, anti-big business, and other liberal groups I could find. I'd even made contact with something called the Undead Urban Alliance which as far as I could figure out was a group fighting for the civil rights of vampires. Who would have thought? I'd also alerted my contacts on the newspapers. They wouldn't care one way or the other about the outcome, but I promised them some fireworks and discomfort among the big boys. That was enough to bring out a handful of reporters looking for blood, or at least a good headline. It had all the makings of a hostile crowd.

The South Sides man made his presentation. It was typical stuff all about progress and the good of the many over the discomfort of a few. The commissioners nodded. A few even pretended to make notes.

Then it was my turn to speak. "South Side has been talking about progress, but when is it progress to turn people out of their homes of a lifetime? How does that serve the public good? This would seem to me to be about profit, not public interest."

Wilson chimed in, "We've offered more than fair compensation."

"And those who wanted to sell did so. But Ms. Smith and Mr. Tolkas don't want to sell, not at any price. South Side owns most of the block. They have plenty of room to build apartment buildings. Why should they need it all?"

"Mr. Njalsson, South Side Development's plans call for a unified design. Leaving the properties in question undeveloped would result in large holes in the façade, spoiling that design."

"So my clients are to be tossed out of their homes so your apartments look pretty?" That brought some cries from the gallery. A few of the commissioners were starting to look a little nervous.

"In any case, your own prospectus states that the development will take place in several phases, over the span of a number of years. Why must you proceed now? By the time you are ready to build on these properties, my clients circumstances may have changed. After all, neither of them is getting any younger."

Wilson took the bait. "While we are willing to concede that Ms. Smith may at some point in the foreseeable future be prepared to move on, as it were, the case of Mr. Tolkas is different for reasons that you well know."

"And what reasons would those be, Mr. Wilson?" I asked facing the gallery.

"Don't play games with me, Njalsson. You know very well the reasons."

"I may, but I'm sure the commissioners and the people in attendance don't. Why don't you inform them?"

"Very well, but remember that you have insisted. Mr. Tolkas is a vampire. He's not going to die any time soon to free up his property because he's already dead."

This brought some cries of bigot from the UUA members in the audience. The commissioners were looking even more nervous.

"And because he's a vampire, his feelings are of no concern?"

"You know as well as I that vampires have no standing under the law. If you force us, we will file on the property as abandoned."

"But how can you say my client has no standing under the law? He's been an employee of the county government for several decades. I have here official pay stubs going back as long as he's been employed. Are you telling me that these payments are to an entity that has no legal standing? I would consider that de facto recognition of my client's existence and his possession of full legal rights."

Wilson was getting flustered now. The galleries had erupted in shouting as various sides tried to be heard. It was clear the commissioners had had enough. The chairman pounded his gavel trying to restore order.

"Mr. Njalsson has raised several points for us to consider. In light of his testimony the commission will postpone any decision on this matter until a later time. This meeting is now adjourned." As a group he and the other commissioners beat a retreat out the back entrance.

Tolkas came up to me and asked, "What does this mean?"

"Well, if nothing else, we've bought ourselves some time. Whatever Rascaski was planning, he now knows that it will face public scrutiny. There may be enough publicity to force him to drop it."

"Do you really believe that?"

"No, but the next move is up to him."

☆　☆　☆　☆　☆

The next few weeks were quiet. The commission scheduled another hearing, postponed it while they waited for a "legal opinion", and then postponed it again. Meanwhile, a few of the papers had picked up the story and just as quickly dropped it when nothing appeared to be happening. My friend on the paper said he was doing a story on Rascaski, but when I asked him how it was going a few weeks later, he said that he was working on something else. He didn't seem to want to talk about it.

South Side made no new legal moves either. I didn't know whether to be relieved or worried. Rascaski didn't seem the type that would give up easily, but for the time being, things seemed to be going smoothly.

I should have known better. Over a month had gone by with no action when I received a call from Tolkas. It was after eleven at night and I was seriously thinking about going to bed.

He sounded agitated, which is something that you don't often see in a vampire. "You've got to get over here. As soon as you can."

"What's up? And where is here?" I asked.

"I'm at my house. I had some visitors from Rascaski. From the old country. I had to deal with them."

The way he said "deal with them" left no doubt what he meant. I took the phrase from the old country to mean that the visitors were vampires, too.

"I don't know who else to turn to. The police aren't going to help."

"Are you ok? Do you think you might have more visitors?"

I found myself talking in code. Tolkas might be right, his phone, or mine, could easily be bugged.

"I'm ok for the moment, but I'm sure there are others outside. You've got to get over here. I'm worried about Gladys Smith."

That threw me. At the hearing, the two had nodded politely, but only in the way that long time neighbors might. They hadn't spoken. And Tolkas had never shown concern for anyone else.

"Look, it'll take me fifteen, twenty minutes to get over there. If there's going to be trouble I need to pick up a friend who's more equipped to handle it. Don't go outside until I get there."

"All right, but hurry," Tolkas said before he hung up.

I was no expert at dealing with vampires, but I suspected that Jack was. I wasn't mistaken. When I called him he said he'd get together a few things and be waiting for me to pick him up. I knew I could count on him.

☆　☆　☆　☆　☆

He was waiting at the curb in front of his shop when I drove up ten minutes later. He was carrying an old carpet bag. He can be a strong as an ox, sometime, but it looked heavy. He swung it into the back seat and climbed in next to me.

"What's in the bag? Holy water, wooden stakes, crucifixes?" I asked.

"You watch too much TV, Egil. But yes, something like that. However, a crucifix will only work if the vampire was a Christian before he became undead. Fire and the sword are more sure. Beheading is best, but hard to do at night if the vampire isn't cooperative." He didn't seem like he was going to add anything else to the list.

It took another five minutes to reach Tolkas's house. All the lights were on. That might have been for my benefit.

I'd read that vampires could see in the dark. I parked the car and we went up to the porch. When I knocked on the door, Tolkas peeked out from behind a blind and then went to the door. While we were waiting I noticed a peculiar man- shaped pattern of dust or ashes on the porch floor.

Jack whispered, "He killed one of them, at least," pointing to the dust with his head.

As I looked at the gruesome remains the phrase "From dust to dust" came to mind. My thoughts were interrupted by Tolkas' opening of the door. He glanced out and then hurried us in, locking the door behind us.

"They started attacking about an hour ago," he said without preamble. "I killed the one out front and two coming in through the cellar. Two more have tried to get in through the rear bedroom window since I called you."

I noticed that his shirt was ripped. He was carrying a sword in his left hand. I'd seen similar swords in gladiator movies. The Romans called it a gladius.

"Why haven't they rushed you all at once?" I asked.

"I'm not sure that Rascaski has that many troops that are willing to risk sacrificing themselves. Immortality, such as it is, is hard to give up. He's probably having to threaten them to get them to act, particularly after I finished the first few off. Also, I don't think he wanted to attract too much attention. He probably didn't think I would put up much of a defense."

As we stood there in the entry hallway a noise came that sounded like it was on the roof. At the same time we could hear footsteps on the front porch.

"Once they get in, it will be harder to fight them off. Do you think you can handle the one on the porch if I go upstairs?"

Jack said, "We can do what must be done," as he pulled what looked like a small battleaxe from his bag. He tossed it to me and then produced another weapon for himself, something that looked like a pirate's cutlass. From the way Jack was holding it, he knew how to use it. He held it in his right hand while he had a large wooden cross in his left. There were two entwined iron nails where the cross piece of the cross met the stem.

"Don't get close if you can avoid it," Jack said. "They are faster than you can imagine and much stronger than a man."

I nodded. My mouth was too dry to speak. Tolkas had already gone upstairs.

The footsteps on the porch had approached the door. It sounded like there were two of them. Suddenly, the door burst in, the chain of the latch breaking. Jack crouched low and his sword leapt out penetrating the torso of the vampire in the doorway. The vampire roared in pain, but it didn't seem to slow him down much. Jack pushed the crucifix in his left hand into the vampire's face as he came into the room. I could smell burning flesh. The cutlass in Jack's hand swung for the neck. The head flew free in the moment before both head and body collapsed into a shower of dust.

The first one had been unarmed, trusting its superhuman strength. The second one was more cautious. He was armed with a sword like a Scottish claymore. He also was six foot four if an inch. Jack backed away from the vampire. Because of his size and the shorter length of his sword he was at least at a foot disadvantage.

All this had happened so fast that I hadn't had a chance to move. Not that I would have. I was petrified. I watched in horror as Jack was being pushed back against the railing of the stairs leading up. He was managing to parry the vampire's sword, but it was evident that he would not be able to hold out against the superior strength and speed for long. Fortunately, in pursuing Jack, he had turned his back towards me giving me an opportunity.

The axe was oddly balanced in my hand, not at all like a wood chopping axe. Instinctively I treated it like a baseball bat, wrapped both hands around the shaft and swung with all my might. It would never have made it out of the park, but the blade cut into the neck. The vampire turned around with a stunned look on his face, and then slumped to the floor. Jack's blade lashed out to complete the job and the body dissolved into a mote of dust like the other.

"How many more do you think there are?" I asked Jack.

"Hard to say. I would not have thought that there were this many," he answered as he tried to get the front door to close again.

Tolkas came down the stairs. His left arm didn't seem to be working. "Good, you got them. I think we had better check on Ms. Smith. From the roof, I think I saw some of Rascaski's men around her house."

"You want to go out there?" I asked. I wasn't too keen on the idea. We'd barely survived our first encounter.

"If all three of us go we'll be safer, but you two can stay here if you like."

He headed for the door. Jack looked at me inquiringly then straightened up to follow. I clutched the axe tightly and followed after Jack. I didn't like it, but I had a feeling we were in this too deeply now to back out. If Rascaski made it through the night he'd be after me.

We marched along the sidewalk towards Gladys Smith's house, Tolkas in the lead, me in the middle watching out to either side and Jack bringing up the rear walking backwards. It was less than eighty feet, but it seemed to take forever. When we got there, the front door was open.

We entered cautiously. The door had been forced. I noted the string of garlic bulbs strung over the entrance. So much for that myth. Or maybe Rascaski had humans working for him as well.

"Ms. Smith? Are you alright?" Tolkas called out. I didn't know if it was wise to announce our presence, but if they were vampires they probably had sensed us anyway. There was no answer.

A quick glance in the parlor showed she wasn't there. We moved towards the back of the house, checking the dining room on the way. She had been in the kitchen when they caught her. A chair was tipped over. There were no signs of blood. The back door of the kitchen was open. It led out onto a small enclosed porch and then into the back yard. The porch door was open, too.

"Where do you think they took her?" I asked. I left the other question unspoken. Was she still alive?

Tolkas stood at the top of the porch steps looking out into the night. He seemed to be sniffing the wind.

Jack still had his bag with him. I hadn't even noticed. He reached in and pulled something out that looked like a cross between a crystal ball and a Leyden jar. Inside there was a needle suspended from a thread. The needle seemed to have a mind of its own spinning around before pointing in one direction.

"Rascaski is that way, and close. I think there's a good chance we'll find Ms. Smith there as well." Jack kept an eye on the needle as he went down the steps into the back yard. As we followed he stopped, then pointed at a large brick house that stood on the other side of the block from us. It backed onto the property between the houses of Tolkas and Ms. Smith. From where we stood, we could see that there was light coming from the cellar windows.

Most of the backyard where we were was an overgrown garden surrounded by a fence. It took a moment in the darkness to find the gate leading onto an alley. We crossed the alley cautiously. To my eyes, it was pitch black. This didn't seem to bother either Jack or Tolkas. I followed along listening to the sound of their feet and trying not to stumble.

The yard of the other house was surrounded by a fence as well, but the gate had been left open. Once in the yard it was easier to see as there was light coming out of the cellar windows. The house stood high off the ground with the cellar half exposed. There were a set of steps leading into the cellar from the yard. They ended in a door with a window. The door was shut, but we could see inside.

There was a small room on the other side of the door. A sink flanked one wall with shelving on the other. At the far end of the room was another door. It was open and showed a brightly lit room beyond. Jack grabbed the handle of the outer door and gently gave it a turn. The door slid open.

Once inside we could hear a voice chanting. I couldn't quite make it out, but it sounded like Latin. It wasn't any Latin that I knew, though, and I had studied the language, both modern and ancient, at CalThaum. Jack seemed to recognize it, though. He didn't seem to like what he heard. He saw the look on my face and whispered, "Archaic Etruscan." How he knew a primitive form of a dead language that no one can speak, I don't know. He does things like that. A lot.

We needn't have bothered being stealthy. Two men came in behind us. From the farther room a voice said, "Good, you're here. Won't you join us? You've saved me the trouble of having to send for you."

The men behind us motioned us forward. There didn't seem to be any point in resisting. They took positions to either side of us. There were three other vampires in the room, all armed. One I took to be Rascaski. The other two made the ones we that we had fought at Tolkas's house look like wimps.

As we entered the room we saw Gladys Smith. She was alive, but she was draped across a large stone set into the floor of the cellar. Ropes bound her hands and feet and her mouth was gagged. The stone had been roughly shaped. Like an altar. Symbols had been inscribed on it and other symbols painted in a circle surrounding it on the floor. I didn't recognize them, and I'd been good in magical symbology — got an A in MS305.

"Archaic Etruscan?" I asked Jack.

"No." He didn't see fit to elaborate, but I could tell he wasn't happy with what he saw. It takes a lot to rattle Jack.

"You really should have sold, Zoltan," Rascaski said. He had been the one chanting. He was wearing a robe sort of thing — blac — just like in the movies. Some vampires have no imagination. "You might have saved yourself and Ms. Smith. Of course I still would have needed a virgin. I would have picked someone younger if I had had my choice."

"What do you need a virgin for?" I asked. I thought that if I could distract him with conversation Tolkas or Jack might think of something.

"I see that your client hasn't told you everything. This neighborhood sits on a place of ancient power. It's centered here, between his house, Ms. Smith's and this one. With the right ritual you can tap into that power. Of course, it can only be done at a certain alignment of the sun, the moon and the earth. That alignment happens tonight. The next time it occurs is in eighteen years. You can see why I couldn't wait for the planning commission. Of course, you need a virgin. Any age will do," he said the last with a smirk.

"I'm surprised you never took advantage of it yourself, Zoltan. You surely were aware of the possibilities. You wouldn't have lived here if you hadn't."

"I never felt the need, Vladimir," Tolkas answered. "I was happy as I was." Strangely, I actually believed him.

"Then you are a fool. But I can't let you delay me any longer. The moment is upon us." He had an ornate dagger carved from obsidian in his hand. He raised it. It didn't take much imagination to figure out what he was going to do with it.

Suddenly, there was a flash of light, then darkness. I heard a cry, sounds of a struggle. I still had my axe, but in the darkness I didn't want to swing it around for fear of hitting Jack or Tolkas.

Gradually the light returned. It wasn't as if the lights had been turned back on, but more as if a masking affect was wearing off. One of the vampires lunged at me. I used my forehand swing with the axe. Either I was getting better at it or he hadn't been expecting me to do anything. His head rolled to the floor before dusting.

Jack had knocked off another one and was holding a third at bay. He was holding something in his left hand, some kind of talisman. I assumed that was what had knocked out the lights.

I finally had a chance to look towards Rascaski. He and Tolkas were engaged hand to hand, Rascaski still armed with the stone knife and Tolkas with his sword clutched in his right hand. Tolkas was at a disadvantage because his left arm was injured, but his right hand held the gladius pointed at Rascaski's eye. Rascaski's knife was aimed at Tolkas's heart. I could see the exertion on both of their faces. Neither was giving an inch.

Suddenly, it was as if Tolkas had pushed forward so that the stone knife entered his chest. Rascaski was caught by surprise and let up. In that moment the sword Tolkas held pierced Rascaski's eye and went straight through into the brain. The two bodies slumped to the ground.

The last vampire turned and ran. I got over to Tolkas. Neither he nor Rascaski had turned into dust. Tolkas eyes were still open, but glazed. Then they cleared for a moment. He wheezed, "The head, cut off his head. Quick before he can recover."

I didn't need to be told twice. A quick stroke of the axe, and Rascaski's body disappeared in a poof of dust.

Tolkas's body lay motionless. Jack came over to look while I freed Ms. Smith. She seemed okay, but shaken. Who could blame her?

"Is he ok?" I asked Jack as he kneeled over the body.

"No, he's gone. The knife is a soul stealer. Not even a vampire could survive its touch."

"Too bad. He was a brave man. One thing I don't understand. At the end it was almost as if he pushed himself onto the blade."

"He did. It was the only way he could see to get Rascaski to let up long enough for him to kill him."

"You mean he sacrificed himself to beat Rascaski?"

"That's exactly what I mean."

"Poor Mr. Tolkas," Gladys Smith said. "He was always such a nice man. Polite, too. And he had such a lovely garden."

Of course, none of this ever came out in the papers. South Side Development just seemed to go away. Gladys Smith still lives in her house. The other houses on the block have been bought up and are being lived in again. They call it urban rejuvenation. There's a young couple living where Tolkas did. They seem to be keeping up the garden.

I heard that Tolkas left some money to the Undead Urban Alliance. I even got my fee from his estate. That set some kind of legal precedent.

I never really liked Tolkas. He was a vampire, after all. Not evil, but not warm and friendly, either. But I have to admire and wonder about him. I can never think about vampires in the same way. A line from Shakespeare's "Merchant of Venice" comes to mind. "If you prick us, do we not bleed?" It just makes you think.

Night Battles

Night Battles

☆　　☆　　☆　　☆　　☆

"I want you to represent my brother, Mr. Njalsson," the woman said from her seat in front of the desk. There was just a hint of an Italian accent to her voice, but her grammar was flawless and indicated both intelligence and education. She was young. Egil guessed her to be in her early to mid twenties, dressed simply in a skirt and sweater and with a minimum of makeup. With thick brown hair that fell to just below her shoulders, hips that were just a touch too wide for her slender frame, and a profile with a shade more character than desirable, she fell just short of what would conventionally be described as beautiful. Pleasant, yes, but not quite beautiful, which just reaffirmed Egil's distrust of conventional standards.

She had come into his office a few minutes earlier, without an appointment, though for a lawyer that was not unusual. People seldom have the foresight to schedule trouble ahead of time, and there was no question that Angelica Maraschino was a woman with troubles. There was also no question that Egil wanted to help her.

"In what way do you want me to represent your brother?" Egil asked.

"He's been accused of maleficium."

Just like that. Not witchcraft, or sorcery, or practicing the Art without a license or any of the dozen other terms for illegal magic in the popular vocabulary. Just maleficium, the precise Latin term for evil doing through the use of magic, one of the most serious crimes on the books relating to the

Art and Science of Magic. The term dated back to Roman times, and had been central to the prosecutions of the Inquisition, but in modern legal usage it was restricted specifically to inducing injury to another human being through the agency of the "dark powers." Until the Supreme Court decision twelve years ago it had been a capital crime in over half the states.

"That's a serious charge, Miss Marachino. It's also an extremely difficult one for the prosecution to prove unless they have very specific types of evidence. I'm no fan of the D.A., but he's not such a fool as to bring a charge of Maleficium without pretty solid proof."

"My brother is innocent, Mr. Njalsson. Pietro is a good man. This is something that I know."

There was a tone of flat assurance in that statement as if it was a fact, and not an opinion. "I take it that you and your brother are quite close?" Egil asked.

"Yes. Since we were little children. Our mother died when we were both very young. That left just the two of us and our father. He was a good parent, but his job — he is a civil engineer — kept him very busy. Pietro and I had a lot of time alone together as we grew up. It was natural that we should become closer than many brothers and sisters. That is one reason why I came to this country to study for my advanced degree, so that I would be close to him."

"You are both from Italy?"

"Yes, from the Friuli in the north, though Pietro is now a citizen of your country. He came here as a university student. He is now a professor of Materials Science at the University.

"And you?"

"I received my undergraduate degree from the University of Bologna, but when I had the opportunity to study here I took it so as to be close to my brother. Our father died two years ago, so I have no close family in Italy. I have been here since the fall semester of last year."

"And you are studying?" Egil asked out of curiosity.

"History. But does that matter?" Angelica asked in puzzlement, "What I am studying?"

"It does to me," Egil replied with a smile. "Seriously, the more I know about your brother, and that includes yourself, the better a defense I can present. Maleficium is a tricky crime to try in the courts from both the prosecution's and the defense's position. Quite a lot of the testimony tends to depend on second hand information and character."

"I see," she said. She looked at him curiously, a smile briefly forming on her lips.

"Tell me, Miss Marachino, why did you come to me? There are quite a few lawyers with more criminal trial experience than myself. I would think you would want one of them, especially on a charge of this seriousness."

"Please, call me Angelica. It is true that there were men of more experience in the law, but you have the reputation of knowing more about the Art than most lawyers. I think that such knowledge will be needed in this case."

"I will do my best, Angelica," Egil said.

"I know you will," she said in a tone that warmed Egil's heart.

"When will I be able to see your brother?"

"I am not sure. He is still being held, and the bail has been set too high for me to raise."

"I'll see if there is something I can do about that."

She thanked him, then left, leaving Egil staring at the door after she had let herself out. It was long moments before he pulled himself together.

Defending a client on a charge of maleficium was serious business, and for more reasons than one he didn't want to lose this case. He was going to have his work cut out for him. It was true that his practice had picked up in the last few years, and with it had come the first signs of material success. He had moved into a new office where the paint was at least firmly attached to the walls. He still couldn't afford a receptionist, but he did have one of the new International Divination Apparatus word processing machines and an answering service, which was a real step up from his early days of struggling. He had also established a reputation for knowing more than just the legal aspects of magic, a holdover from his days as a student in applied metaphysics at the California Institute of Thaumaturgy before he had switched to the law under the mistaken impression that he'd make more money. But his work to date had mostly been in the civil aspects of magic: warrantees, contracts, negligence. He'd done very little criminal work in the last two years, and certainly nothing as major as a case of maleficium.

He pulled down a few key books from his small legal library, the State Statutes, a couple of commentaries. The information he obtained was scarcely encouraging. He'd been correct about the legal definition. The relevant statute defined Maleficium as causing injury to another human being through the agency of the dark forces. The injury had to be direct and physical. Property was excluded by the definition. The "dark forces" were explicit, too. Simple witchcraft, curses, and the practice of voodoo were all lesser crimes. Also excluded were injury either intentional or accidental through the use of either "white" or "green" magics. At the root of the definition was the fact that maleficium involved not the Half World of normal magic, but "black magic", that is, dealing with demons of the Dark World. It was this fact, the involvement of demons, which made the crime so serious.

The commentaries had little to add. The first seemed to draw heavily on the Malleus Maleficarum, the manual of the Inquisition.   Though the author traced the legal trends through the discovery of the scientific principles of magic in the nineteenth century to the present day, he seemed to be of the opinion that anyone even suspected of dealing in maleficium should be burned at the stake. He produced a plethora of precedents to support his case.

The second author was more liberal in his outlook. He denied that there even was such a crime as maleficium on the grounds that there was no legal precedent establishing the reality of dealings with the Dark World or even its very existence. As such matters were strictly forbidden under law; the lack of documentation was not surprising. Egil could put little trust in this author as his own experience had proved to him the reality of demons. Nonetheless, he would make full use of the arguments presented if nothing better materialized.

It seemed that as always happened in cases involving the more infamous aspects of the Art he would have to consult other sources. However, there would be time enough to contact Old Jack later. His first order of business would have to be interviewing his client and seeing if he could manage his release.

Egil saw Pietro Marachino at the county jail in the room reserved for lawyers' conferences. Angelica's brother was taller, had lighter colored hair and looked to be four or five years older, but the family resemblance was strong. He seemed young to be a professor, but judging from his sister, theirs had been a well educated family.

"Call me Peter, it's simpler," he said upon introduction in an accent somewhat heavier than his sister, though his English had the same fluency. Egil judged that under better circumstances he would have been quite charming. Now he just sounded worried.

"Angelica arranged for you to represent me?" Marachino asked.

"If you want me to," Egil replied.

"I trust Angelica's judgment. She's a bright girl."

"I agree with you," Egil said drawing a quizzical look from Marachino, "but this is a serious matter. I have to tell you that I haven't had much experience in criminal law, not on such a serious charge. If you have any reservations about my representing you feel free to make other arrangements for counsel."

"You seem unusually honest for a lawyer," Marachino said with a smile. "Perhaps that's what I need. My sister explained to me that you had expertise in matters outside the law. I think that that expertise may be important in my case."

"You do realize how serious the charge is, don't you?"

"I am not an expert on American law, no. But I know how the matter would be treated in Italy," Marachino said with resignation.

"Twenty years ago you would be facing the electric chair in this state. Since the Supreme Court ruling that has been reduced to life imprisonment for cases resulting in death, twenty years otherwise. There is also the factor that you were not born in this country. It is possible that, if convicted, your naturalization might be revoked and you could be deported. I want you to understand all the possibilities up front."

"I see." Anxiously he asked, "What would be my sister's status if the later should happen."

"It's hard to say. It would depend on the immigration service and her visa. I'd say that the chances would not be good for her staying in this country. I can understand your concern, but I think that you should be worrying more about a long prison term for yourself." Egil didn't like the idea of Angelica leaving, at least not yet, but it was her brother, not her, that he was representing.

"I am afraid that I can't stop worrying about my sister," Pietro said spreading his hands wide. "I am all she has in the way of family. I had hoped that when she received her degree she would settle here in America. There is nothing for her at home, especially if her brother should be convicted of witchcraft. Italy is much more closed minded about such matters, especially in the Friuli."

"Perhaps then it would be best all the way around if you were not convicted," Egil said. He liked the way that Marachino was more concerned for his sister than himself, but it bothered him that his client seemed resigned to the possibility of being found guilty. It was a bad sign. "Maybe we should concentrate on that."

"Si. Yes you are right. Where should we begin?"

"With the basics. The alleged victim in this case is one Bastian Magnossi. Do you know him?"

"No, not as such," Pietro answered haltingly.

"What does that mean?" Egil asked sharply. "Do you know him under another name?"

"I don't know. I mean I don't know if I know him at all."

Egil wasn't satisfied, but decided to go on. "He seems to know you. Can you think of any reason why he might accuse you of an act of maleficium? A business reason? Something personal? Something involving your sister?"

"No," Marachino said slapping his hands down hard on the table. "Angelica has no part in this. She is not involved in any way."

Egil sat back in his chair and looked at his client. Marachino was breathing hard, but otherwise was under control. If anything, it was a look of sadness, not anger that was in his eyes.

"Look, Peter. I'm your lawyer. Communications between us is privileged. I cannot be made to testify. I think there is something that you're not telling me. If I'm going to defend you, I need to know what it is."

"No, there is nothing to tell. I am innocent, Mr. Njalsson. I am not a strega. Believe me."

"It doesn't matter what I believe, Mr. Marachino. It's what a jury believes."

"Yes. I know," Marachino said with the same tone of resignation he had used earlier.

"We can go over this later," Egil said, seeing that there were no immediate prospects of clarification. "The most important thing is to get you out of here."

"The bail is too high. I don't have that kind of money."

"Two hundred thousand is a bit steep. I should be able to get that reduced. Do you have any property, any assets that we can post for a bond?"

"No property. I live in an apartment. I'm just an assistant professor and not that for very long. All I have is my car and some stock left from my father's estate. But if something should happen to me, Angelica will need that."

"I think your sister can take care of herself. It's more important to get you out on bail. It will look bad if you can't raise it. A client in jail is damning to a jury."

"If I am not damned already," Marachino said quietly as Egil signaled the guard that his interview was finished.

Egil hadn't liked the way things had gone. There was something bothering Angelica's brother, something related to the case, but he couldn't put his finger to. One thing was certain; there hadn't been the smell of sorcery about him. Egil wasn't a trained witchsmeller, but he had had run-ins with the Black Arts before. Marachino didn't seem to fit the psychological mold for a witch, either. He was disturbed, but if Egil was a judge, it was some inner demon eating at him, not contact with the Dark World.

☆   ☆   ☆   ☆   ☆

It was too late to get the bail reduced that day. It would probably take a couple of days, at least, if the court was willing. Besides, he was feeling out of his depths on this one. The whole business of maleficium was a shadowy one, an area that he was only passingly familiar with. He felt the need for more information.

His destination was not the law library, but a place much more disreputable. From the outside it looked like a seedy second hand shop that didn't do much business. However, in some quarters it did have a certain reputation, only not for antiques.

The shop was dark, though the front door wasn't locked. Egil let himself in, then walking slowly to avoid stumbling over the clutter of the shop headed towards the light coming from a door at the back of the shop.

"Jacob, are you here?" Egil called out.

There was the scraping of a chair and then footsteps before an old man with longish hair and a beard appeared in the light. "Egil, Junge," Jacob said in a Yiddish accent, "I've got a customer now, but if you can wait a few minutes I can see you."

"Fine," Egil said. The "customer" was probably an old woman having her fortune told, the real business of the shop. Egil had met the proprietor when he had defended him on a charge of practicing magic without a license some years earlier. He'd lost, but won the friendship of "Old Jack", as he had been known then.

"Just go on back and I'll be with you as soon as I can."

Egil nodded and headed towards the sanctum sanctorum.

In contrast to the front of the shop, the study was neat and organized. Shelves of books lined two of the walls while apparatus and jars of mysterious content lined a third. Egil had examined the library before and knew that the books were in at least a dozen languages that he could recognize and a few that he could not. Quite a few were several centuries old, a compendium of learned magic that rivaled most university libraries. Surprisingly, a goodly portion of the works were more modern texts, some of the more technical of which Egil found as opaque as those in Chinese or Egyptian. He also knew that Jack, or Jacob, as he was styling himself these days, was conversant with the entire collection.

His friend was a mystery, even to Egil; something that he never managed to clear up. Not that he wasn't willing to talk about himself. He would do so endlessly if primed. The problem was that the stories were never consistent. At various times Jacob had claimed to be a druid, a gypsy, a Hindu swami, a defrocked priest, a Finnish sorcerer, an Arab mystic, and a Tibetan monk. Currently his claim was that he was a rabbi from Bohemia, hence the name change to Jacob pronounced Yah cobe. To make matters even more confusing, he seemed capable of producing detailed knowledge of all his various identities, details that Egil had never been able to prove false. This was more amazing as the recollections spanned an era almost as great as that spanned by the books in the library.

He had even offered as proof the occasional odd photograph or tintype, usually of a group of men posed against some identifying background, one of whom bore at least a superficial resemblance to Jack. The fact that the pictures were spread over a century and four continents was left unexplained. Egil had never been able to decide whether the pictures were legitimate, an outright fraud, or the delusion of an old man. He had noticed lately that in the photo of a dozen rabbis and rabbinical students standing in front of a Polish synagogue, one of the rabbis looked very much like Jacob. The resemblance had never seemed so striking before, though he had seen the picture dozens of times. It was dated Cracow, 1897. That made him wonder about the faded photo of the tree Tibetan monks and their yak.

The one thing he was certain of was that Jacob knew more about magic than any man he had ever met before, particularly in those areas outside the limits of modern scientific technology. This knowledge encompassed not only "white" and "green" magic but included the lore of the Dark World, "black" magic, as well. Jacob had never practiced black magic to Egil's knowledge, but he was conversant with the means of protecting against it, lore that was not available in any university that Egil knew of.

While he waited, Egil searched the books for one particular volume, the Malleus Maleficarum. He found it in three editions; one in Latin, one German, and one in English. His Latin was rusty, as was his seventeenth century German, the publishing date of that version. The English was a modern translation scarcely fifty years old. He was thumbing through it when Jacob came in.

"That's rubbish. Complete rubbish. Pure invention by an ignorant priest. Pure propaganda," Jacob said as he sat down in the ancient easy chair under the lamp in the corner.

Egil stuffed the book back in its place on the shelf. "If it's rubbish, why do you have three editions, all valuable for their age if nothing else?"

"Because, my boy, that book was at the core of the persecutions of the Inquisition. In those days it paid to know your enemy. Why the interest? Is the state going to bring back the rack and thumbscrews?"

"In a way. I'm defending a case of maleficium. I admit I'm a little vague on the background. I barely passed History of Magic at CalThaum," Egil answered.

"Maleficium?" Jacob asked quizzically. "A serious matter if true. You should be careful. Is your client guilty?"

"I'm not sure. That's what bothers me. I find it hard to believe that he's guilty. He's just not the type, but there is some type of involvement. I don't think that he's guilty of maleficium, but he's guilty of something, at least in his own mind." Egil went on to explain the details of the case.

Jacob nodded sagely during the account without saying anything until Egil had finished. "So you think this Pietro is innocent because you like his sister? There could be worse reasons, I think."

"That's part of it," Egil said blushing, "but only part. I didn't get the smell of the Dark World when I talked to Marachino."

"So, you are learning something after all. You do have something of the sense about you, my boy. It's too bad that school got to you first."

"I'm a lawyer, not a magician," Egil said defensively.

"True," Jacob shrugged. "Well we all have our own shame to bear. You say your client was born in the Friuli? Do you know if his family had been in the region long?"

"Not for sure, but I got the impression that they were an old family of some note in the region. Why? Do you think it's relevant?"

"It's possible," Jacob said. "Are you familiar with the benandanti?"

"Benandati? No, can't say that I am. It means something like do gooders, doesn't it?" Egil asked.

"Well farers might be a better translation, but that is the general idea. It was a cult of the sixteenth and seventeenth centuries in the mountainous north region of Italy, of which the Friuli is part. The cult itself may have been much older, pagan times possibly, but the sixteenth century was when it came under the scrutiny of the Inquisition."

"And this cult engaged in Maleficium?" Egil asked.

"Nein, nein. Just the opposite. The members of the cult always alleged that their purpose was to fight witchcraft. Hence the term benandanti, 'do gooder' as you put it. The roots seem to have been a sort of pagan agricultural ritual to insure good harvests by fighting evil in the form of witches who cursed the crops."

"If they were good, why the interest of the Inquisition?"

"Don't be simple, Egil. This was in the sixteenth century before your science had recognized the validity of magic. It was also the time of the Reformation. Anything that didn't fit into the scheme of the Church smacked of heresy to the authorities, and it was the Church's job, not a bunch of unlettered vigilantes, to protect the population from evil. The repression of the Inquisition was as much political as religious, and the benandanti were too independent for the Church's liking."

"So you think Marachino might be part of a latter day cult of these benandanti?"

"A possibility," Jacob said with a shrug. "Only a possibility. But the Friuli is a mountainous region largely isolated even into this century. Such a cult could have remained active if underground. It wouldn't hurt to look into the background of this other man, the victim, as he claims. Find out his antecedents. Could it be he comes from the Friuli, too?"

"It's a starting place, at least," Egil said. "I need to know more about these benandanti. I don't remember reading anything about them when I was in college."

"Not surprising. Not much appeared in literature until the last decade or so. There is a book by an Italian, Carlo Ginzburg. I Benandanti: Stregoneria e culti agrari tra Cinquecento e Siecento."

"I don't read Italian very well," Egil commented.

"Then it's time you learned," Jacob said, "particularly if you continue your interest in your client's sister. But there is a translation. Up there on the second shelf from the top, right hand. Yes, that's it."

Egil picked the book off the shelf. "Anything else I should know?"

"Just this. Even if your client is benandanti, someone is a witch. Be careful."

"Thanks for the warning. I will be. Thanks for the book."

Jacob gave a little cough and then said, "Aren't you forgetting something?"

Egil smiled, then pulled out a pint bottle of peppermint schnapps from his jacket pocket. He handed it to Jacob who twisted off the cap and took a good swallow. In his earlier incarnation as Jake it had been Irish whiskey, but the thirst had been the same.

"Mazl tov," Jacob said after a second pull on the bottle.

Egil spent most of the night reading the book Jacob had given him. At the heart of the cult of the benandanti was their belief that they could, at certain times, leave their bodies in the middle of the night and travel, often under the direction of a captain, to some distant place. While they traveled so in spirit, their bodies remained behind inanimate. The purpose of these nocturnal travels was to meet at some location and there do battle with a group of witches who were in a similar spirit state. The agrarian symbolism was apparent; the chief weapon of the benandanti being fennel stalks which they used to beat the witches. If they were successful in the battle the witches were defeated and could not work their evil which was generally aimed at crops or the products of the harvest such as beer or wine which the witches would try to spoil. Under the persecution of the Inquisition the nature of the cult changed, debased by the pressure of the inquisitors into the very image of the accusations against it, but at root its members had truly believed that they were performing a service to their community.

It was an interesting piece of history of the Art, but unable to see how it fit into his case, Egil turned to more pressing matters. He spent most of the morning working on bail arrangements which included a request for a bail reduction hearing. The judge granted this, but couldn't fit it into his schedule until the following day, justice in this case being anything but swift.

Knowing it was the best he could do, Egil phoned Angelica with the news. It seemed to cheer her up, and Egil found himself melting at the tone of gratitude in her voice. He was still bothered by the suspicion that his client was concealing something from him. Thinking that his sister might shed some light on the matter, Egil asked if he could see her later to ask her some questions. He wanted to get to her before her brother was released. He had a feeling that she might be less forthcoming after talking to him. She agreed to meet with him and a time was set up.

Egil arrived at her apartment just after five. Angelica greeted him at the door. It was a pleasant place, not large, but with a wide set of windows on one end of the living room that opened out onto a view of the park along the river. It was not extravagant, but it looked to be more than typical for graduate student's digs.

"Nice place," Egil said noncommittally.

"It's really my brother's. When I came to this country I moved into the second bedroom. I was planning to get a place of my own, but this is so convenient to the university. Besides, I think we both liked the feeling of being a family that living together gives us."

"You both seem to be close. When I saw your brother yesterday he seemed more worried about you than himself."

"Pietro is like that. The big brother. Especially now that Papa has died. Perhaps a little overprotective at times," she said with a sad smile, "but I think I need that a little."

"Have you seen your brother?" Egil asked.

"Only once," Angelica replied. "He does not think that jail is a proper place for a young woman. I think that he is ashamed of being a prisoner."

"There's nothing to be ashamed of yet. He's innocent until proven guilty," Egil said.

"He will be proven innocent, won't he?"

"That's for the jury to decide, but I'm going to do my best to see that the verdict is not guilty. You may be able to help me. Your brother wasn't very communicative when I interviewed him yesterday. If I could ask you some questions?"

"Of course. Anything I can do to help."

"Did your brother ever mention a Bastian Magnossi?" Egil asked.

Angelica thought for a moment, then replied, "No. Not that I can recall. That's the man who was supposedly the victim, isn't he?"

"Yes," Egil confirmed. "The name has no associations at all?"

"No. Wait," she said after a hesitation. "There was a Magnossi family where we grew up. I don't remember a Bastion, though. In fact we didn't know them, really. They were just a family, and it was not such a big place that you didn't at least know people's names. It's possible that he might be related, or it could just be a coincidence. Is that important?"

"Who knows. It could be," Egil said. "So far there doesn't seem to be any connection between him and your brother. No motive either for your brother to want to hurt him, or for Magnossi to make a false charge against your brother. People don't usually make accusations about total strangers."

"I still have some friends in the Friuli. I could call them and ask if they know something about this man or his family. Would that help?"

"It might. Please do that," Egil said. "Other than this Magnossi, did your brother have any enemies, people with professional jealousies, any sort of motive someone might have to discredit him, anything like that?"

"No, not that I can think of. His colleagues seem to think well of him. My brother is a very likable person."

"Maybe a disgruntled student?"

"No, not that I know of. I think he was a good teacher. He has a lot of patience with people. More so than I," she said with a smile. Egil decided that she was very pretty when she smiled. It seemed to suit her personality more than worry.

"Nothing strange about his personal life? Girlfriends, anything like that?"

"No. He had no one that he was seeing regularly, though he went out frequently enough. He is handsome, and can be very charming in an Italian sort of way which I think American women find attractive, but I think that he was very careful about not seeing women who might misunderstand his attentions. Also, he is not the kind of person who likes to hurt people. He is very careful of other people's feelings."

"You know your brother better than I do, but I agree with you. He is not a person who hurts others."

Egil gathered his thoughts for a minute then asked, "Before he was arrested, did he give any signs of anxiety? Did it seem that anything was bothering him? Any unusual behavior?"

"No. He seemed very happy. He enjoys his work, enjoys his life," Angelica answered.

Egil was trying to think of another line of questioning when she said, "There was one strange incident. It happened about a month ago. I had gone out with some friends to a party. I got home late and Pietro had already gone to bed. He worries if I stay out late, so I thought I'd see if he was up and tell him that I was home. I went into his bedroom and I saw him lying in his bed, but it was very strange. Usually when a person is sleeping, they move around a little, but he was completely still except for his breathing. Even that was very shallow. There was no tossing or any sort of movement. It was almost frightening. I thought he might be ill, or had some sort of attack. I tried to wake him, but I couldn't rouse him. I got very worried, sat up in a chair next to his bed for hours. He didn't move in all that time. Then, a little before dawn his body seemed to relax and he rolled over. I felt a little foolish then, and went to bed. When I got up in the morning it was as if nothing ever happened. I asked him how he felt, and he said fine. I didn't press him. He can be a little vain about his machismo, and I wasn't sure that he would approve of me sitting by his bed all night as if I was his nurse."

"That's all?" Egil asked.

"Yes. Why, should there be more?" Angelica queried.

"I don't know. It does seem a little unusual, but I guess I don't know too much about sleep disorders. Maybe he was just having a dream."

"Perhaps. I've heard that in the dream state the motor centers of the brain cease to work so that the dreamer doesn't injure himself. But I didn't think that dreams lasted so long."

"You're probably right. It was just a dream," Egil said. Then, trying to do so in an offhand manner he asked, "Tell me, are you familiar with the term benandanti?"

"Benandanti?" she said quizzically. "Yes. They were a cult in the Friuli in sixteenth century. It's not my period of study, but I have read something of it. The old women used to talk about it a little when I was a child, though in a pretty distorted fashion. You know, how folk legends get distorted after a few centuries. They used the benandanti to scare little children into behaving. Like a strega, a witch."

"Does this have something to do with my brother's case?" she asked. "Do you think this Magnossi is part of some sort of witch cult?"

"No, not really. It's just something that came up while talking to a friend of mine when I mentioned that you were from the Friuli. He's something of an expert on the history of magic and witchcraft."

She dropped it then, and after pleasantries Egil offered to take her to dinner. She said that she didn't feel up to it, but said that she could cook something up for him. It was some hours and a bottle of Bardolino later that Egil left, having come to the conclusion that Angelica's talents for cooking were a match for her other charms.

☆   ☆   ☆   ☆   ☆

Egil finally arranged for the bail reduction hearing the following morning. The presiding judge, one Harold Griswell and as grim as his name, was not one to start matters before ten, thus giving Egil time for breakfast at the coffee shop in the basement of the court house. The customers were sparse at that time of the morning, and Egil, recognizing a friend, sat next to him at the counter and ordered coffee and a Danish. Police Sergeant Joseph O'Neil looked unnatural in civvies, especially as the sport coat was too tight and his face was shaved almost raw in an effort to look respectable. He had managed only to look like a policeman about to testify in court.

"What brings my favorite flatfoot to court?" Egil asked.

"Oh, hi counselor," the cop said grinning sheepishly. "I'm testifying in the Hernandez case."

"That the one where the pimp worked a spell on his hookers' tricks so they went away without services rendered, as it were?"

"Nice turn of phrase, counselor, and a neat trick it was. Hernandez got himself some mojo dust that put the marks in a trance. They'd wake up a couple of hours later none the wiser and meanwhile Hernandez's stable, not having to deal with the messy intermediaries, were out turning more tricks. Why, he had some of his girls doing four, five tricks an hour."

"What are they charging him with, false advertising?" Egil asked out of professional curiosity.

"No, though they should be, shouldn't they?" O'Neil said laughing at the joke. "Dealing in controlled substances and witching without consent. If you ask me, the marks deserved what they got. A few bucks lighter and no lasting harm."

"I'm not so sure about that. Voodoo can be nasty stuff. There's a lot of black magic mixed in. That's why it's so powerful."

"Well, you know a lot more about that stuff than I do. Or care to either," O'Neil shrugged.

"Just be on your guard that Hernandez doesn't start sticking pins in dolls and putting a curse on you."

"Geez. You don't think he could do that, counselor, do you?" the cop asked suddenly alarmed.

"Probably not," Egil said, suddenly ashamed of himself. Voodoo, to be successful, required a strong belief on the part of the victim as well as possession of something from the body of the victim such as hair or nail clippings. The strongest spells required blood. Voodoo was primarily Sympathetic Magic which was why it was usually limited to the Haitian community where the evoked ties were strongest. "But to play it safe, I'd burn or bury any nail clippings or hair cuttings."

"Thanks for the advice, I'll do that, though the missus will probably think I'm crazy. If I can ever do anything for you, just ask."

"Sure, don't mention it."

"What you here for, anyway?" O'Neil asked wanting to change the subject.

"Bail reduction hearing. The Marachino case," Egil answered.

"Yeah, I heard about that one," O'Neil said. "Bastian Magnossi's the victim. Ain't that a laugh?"

"You know him?" Egil asked quizzically.

"Yeah, every cop on the force does. We've been trying to pin something on him for years, but nothin's ever stuck. He runs an extortion racket, or so we think. No proof, but a lot of shop keepers and small businessmen are paying him money for something."

"Interesting, Joe. Tell me more."

"Not much to tell. Like I said, no proof. Just when one of these businessmen decides not to pay they suddenly have an accident, like all the food in a restaurant spoils over night, things like that. One guy, a beer distributor, had a whole warehouse of beer go sour on him. But nothing to pin on Magnossi. No signs of forced entry, no physical evidence. Nothing to implicate Magnossi or any of his stooges."

"Magic?"

"You got me, counselor. There wasn't anything the forensic boys could find, but then, none of them is really a first-rate wizard. If they were, they wouldn't be working for the city. Sorry I can't help you out."

"Don't worry about it," Egil said. "You may have given me more than you know."

"Well, if you get anything on Magnossi, just give me a call. I'd be happy to bust him."

"I'll remember that. Well, I've got to run. Be seeing you."

☆   ☆   ☆   ☆   ☆

When Egil entered the courtroom, Angelica was sitting in the front row. She smiled as he took the seat next to her.

"Will you be able to arrange bail?" she asked.

"Depends. Griswell isn't an easy judge, but he is fair. I'm not sure how far the prosecution wants to push it. I think the chances are good," Egil said trying to sound more confident than he felt. Griswell was also known to be less than sympathetic to the Art. Rumor had it that he favored bringing back burning at the stake in cases of black magic.

There were a couple of other pieces of business before the court that morning. Egil used the time to check out the opposition. The prosecutor turned out to be Arnold, which was a stroke of good luck. Arnold was competent, but no ball of fire. He also wasn't out to make a name for himself. He wouldn't be out for blood. What worried him was the man with whom he was conferring. The sight of him raised the hackles on the back of Egil's neck. He was blonde but with a complexion too dark to be Scandinavian. Almost too handsome, he was taller than average, though not intimidatingly so. What struck Egil was the icy stare from the pale blue eyes. He was no witch smeller, but he sensed an evil in that man. He nudged Angelica to point him out, but she was unable to identify him.

"The People versus Marachino," the bailiff announced. Egil took his place as his client was ushered in by one of the guards.

Arnold made the first presentation. As fitting his style, it was a lackluster recounting of the seriousness of the crime and the foreign birth of the accused. He made the expected motion that bail not be reduced at that time. The brevity of his remarks indicated that the D.A. wasn't all that serious about keeping the bail high. That made Egil wonder a bit about the strength of their case.

"I trust that the defense has a motion to make," Griswell quipped dryly.

"Yes, your Honor," Egil replied as he stood.

"I would like to point out to the court that while my client was born in Italy, he is a naturalized citizen of this country. Also, he is a man with a profession and a reputation, something that he would not abandon lightly. As the prosecution has produced no reason to indicate that my client would fail to appear for his trial I move that he be released on his own recognizance."

"These are serious charges, Mr. Njalsson, I'm sure you will agree," Griswell intoned from the bench. "However, I note your points about the accused's professional reputation and citizenship." He said that last with emphasis indicating his disapproval of the prosecution's appeal to prejudice. "I therefore reduce bail to fifty thousand dollars or a ten thousand dollar property bond. Is that acceptable counselors?"

Arnold made no objection and Egil gave his assent. It was as much as he had hoped for. The judge scribbled his signature on the papers and asked for the next case. Egil had come prepared for this eventuality and made the arrangements with the clerk. In a few minutes his client was free and was leaving the courtroom with his sister.

They had gotten out into the hallway when they met the man who had been talking to Arnold. At first Marachino had a look of complete surprise as if he had seen a ghost, then his expression turned to hatred. The other man returned the hate, though his anger was cold and calculating in nature. Egil could feel his client tense up, ready for a fight. His sister looked on with bewilderment and alarm. Quickly the lawyer put his hand around Marachino's arm and pulled him down the corridor. Only when he had gotten both of them in the elevator and the doors had shut did Marachino start to relax.

"Who was that?" Egil asked sharply.

"I've never met him before in my life," Pietro answered. It wasn't an evasion, but Egil didn't think it was the whole story.

"Are you in the habit of glaring at complete strangers?"

"No," his client replied angrily, then more calmly, "No."

"Well, then who is he?"

"I think that must be Bastian Magnossi," Marachino said shaking his head.

"Then you do know him?"

"No, we've never met. Let's get out of this place."

Egil drove the two of them back to their apartment. Pietro sat sullenly in the back seat. Angelica sat in the front looking worried. Egil kept silent and paid attention to his driving.

When they got to the apartment his client disappeared into his bedroom. Moments later they could hear a shower being run. Angelica offered to make him a drink, though it seemed she was more interested in having something to do then being a good hostess.

"What's wrong with him?" she asked.

"I take it he's not normally like this?" Egil asked in return.

"No, never. Pietro is almost embarrassingly easy going. He never gets angry. I've never seen this side of him. It's just not like him at all."

After that she didn't say anything at all. Egil was on the verge of leaving when her brother reappeared from his bedroom. The tension had drained from him and as he mixed a drink for himself he apologized for his earlier behavior, showing some of the European charm Angelica had claimed for him.

"I am sorry, Mr. Njalsson. You must understand what an ordeal this has been for me and my sister."

"I understand completely," Egil said in his best reassuring professional tone. "I've been through situations like this before with other clients. I know what a shock the first exposure to the criminal justice system can be."

"Yes," Marachino answered, "it is not an experience to be desired."

"If you feel up to it, I do have a few questions that I'd like to ask to prepare your defense."

"Yes, alright," he answered absentmindedly.

"What do you know about the benandanti?"

"Benandanti?" his client answered suddenly defensive. "Why do you ask? I know nothing of these things. It is all superstition."

"You're sure?" Egil pressed.

"Yes. I have said so, haven't I?" he replied. "These matters are distressing my sister. Can we deal with this another time?"

"Of course," Egil answered, though it wasn't Angelica who seemed distressed. "Well, I have some other work to attend to. If there's nothing else I can do for you right now I'll be on my way."

Angelica came over to see him out. Her hand was on her brother's arm as if to reassure him, but the smile that she gave was for Egil. As he left, the lawyer had a lot on his mind.

After office hours Egil stopped off at Jacob's. He still didn't have any idea of the kind of defense he was going to put up, and so far his client was being singularly unhelpful. What he did know was that somehow the benandanti cult was at the root of it and supplied the tie between Marachino and Magnossi. Therefore, he wasn't surprised that he found himself relying again on the wisdom of his sorcerous acquaintance.

Jacob was making supper for himself in the kitchen of the apartment above the shop. He seemed to be paying more attention to the bottle of schnapps on the counter than to the sausages he was preparing, but then that wasn't unusual. Egil helped himself to a beer from the refrigerator while he updated his friend on the case.

"Ja. It is all of one piece."

"Then you think that Marachino and Magnossi are mixed up in a benandanti cult."

"No, of course not. You are not thinking," Jacob scolded. "The purpose of the benandanti is to fight evil. Evil in the form of witches. If Marachino is benandanti then this Magnossi must be a strega. A witch. Good guy, bad guy. And your client is the good guy. Or the other way around."

"No, I don't think so. This Magnossi struck me as a bad egg. I could almost feel the evil," Egil said.

"You should have felt it. That is your trouble. That fancy smancy school you went to took all the good sense out of you. The biggest part of the Art is feeling. If you can't feel good and evil then you're in big trouble and shouldn't involve yourself with magic."

"That's why I'm a lawyer," Egil defended himself.

"Well I won't say it's a waste, because you are a good lawyer even if you couldn't get me off, but you also have the makings of a good wizard if you'd work at it and forget all the junk you learned in school."

"Never mind that," Egil said trying to keep Jacob from wandering off the subject. "It makes some sense to me now. This Magnossi is running some kind of protection racket, and from what Joe told me he's probably using the black art to do his dirty work which is why the cops can't pin anything on him."

"Now you're thinking," Jacob said flopping the potatoes and sausages out onto a plate.

"Right. And Marachino as a benandanti has been trying to stop him which has been putting the heat on Magnossi. So Magnossi, to get Marachino off his back, frames him."

'Maybe, maybe not," Jacob said with a shrug.

'What do you mean?"

'Your client, if he is benandanti, has been using magic to harm Magnossi. That is the nature of the cult. It might not be necessary to fake evidence. It might already exist. But it won't be maleficium, because benandanti practice white magic, not black."

"Are you sure of that? I mean in the legal sense," Egil asked.

"You're the big shot lawyer, not me. I'm just an old junk dealer. But the difference between white and black magic can be proved if you know how, which I do, even if those so called professional wizards can't tell the difference between black magic and mustard — speaking of which, will you get the mustard from the refrigerator when you get yourself another beer?"

"I'll pass on the beer," Egil said as he dug the mustard out of refrigerator and put it on the table. "I've got some legal research to do on this angle. If Marachino was acting to prevent a crime and using white magic then maybe his actions were legal."

"Ja, you do that," Jacob said turning his attention to the sausages. "And try looking in Blackmore's The Art and the Law, particularly the case of the Queen vs. Dee in 1893. There's a copy in my library downstairs if you don't have one."

Egil knew better than to be surprised at either Jacob's library or his knowledge of anything pertaining to the Art. Instead, he went down to the library to search out Blackmore.

Other business occupied Egil for the next few days, though not so much that he didn't manage to squeeze in a dinner date with Angelica. As no trial date having been set, he put the case on the back burner to catch up on his defense of a misappropriation of trade secrets being brought by Continental Magic against a wizard who had left their employ and formed a business of his own to exploit a new spell useful in the pharmaceutical industry. The wizard had been a classmate of Egil's at CalThaum. Continental's case had little merit, but they could afford a bevy of east coast lawyers who specialized in squashing the entrepreneurial urges of Continental's employees. Egil was no match for their legal talent, but he was basing the defense on technical issues, a sound approach in the circumstances, but a difficult one that required a lot of research and background work on his part.

It was while immersed in this problem that he received a call from Arnold, the prosecutor in Angelica's brother's case.

"I just thought I'd let you know, Njalsson, that the state won't be prosecuting the case against your client," Arnold said over the telephone.

"Is this some kind of joke?" Egil said incredulously. "You arrest my client on one of the most serious crimes in the book, damage his reputation almost beyond repair, and now you say that you're not prosecuting, just like that. Is there something I should know, or should I be thinking of bringing charges of false arrest here?"

"Look, we've got a situation here. We thought we had reason to proceed in this case, but now our star witness is refusing to testify. Without him we don't have a case. The D.A.'s office can't see wasting either of our times on the other evidence we got. Frankly, I think it's in your client's best interest to let the matter drop. He's involved in something that ain't kosher, but without our witness, we can't prove a thing. Let's just leave it at that."

"This witness of yours wouldn't happen to be Bastian Magnossi, would it?" Egil asked sarcastically.

"I can't tell you that, that's confidential," Arnold say. "Let's just say that in light of the alleged victim's reputation this office isn't overly enthusiastic about proceeding on his behalf if he's not willing to cooperate. So, your boy gets off. Okay?"

"Yeah. Okay. Thanks for calling, Arnold," Egil said, then hung up. Arnold was straight arrow and a pretty decent guy, so Egil didn't suspect him of pulling any tricks, but there was some funny business going on that he didn't care for. On the other hand, the interests of his client, and his relationship with Angelica, would probably best be served by letting the case die a quiet death. No matter what the verdict, Marachino's reputation would suffer if it went to trial. As it was, Marachino was free, and Egil would collect a small fee, maybe another date with his sister, and could get back to work on the Continental Magic case.

Several weeks went by after that.   Pietro Marachino went back to his work at the university. Angelica resumed her studies. Egil spent a good portion of his time fighting the legal tactics Continental was using in the case against his friend. They had asked for a change in venue for the trial which would have put a real burden on both his client and himself. They had also asked for an injunction barring his client from exploiting his work until the case was settled. This would have undoubtedly forced his company into bankruptcy had not the judge ruled against both motions. Egil was winning the opening rounds in the case, but it was keeping him busy. Still, he was managing to see Angelica as often as his schedule permitted.

All in all, things were going well, which was why an anguished call from Pietro Marachino caught him by surprise.

"Please, Egil, you must come over here at once," Pietro had told him over the phone. "It is Angelica. She needs help, and you are the only one I can turn to. Please come."

It didn't take much pleading to convince Egil, despite the fact that he had just gotten to bed after a long day in court. He was already grabbing his pants by the time that he hung up the phone.

Before he left, Egil grabbed his bag of "magic tricks" from its place of neglect at the back of the front closet. It contained the tools of a working wizard, some were remnants of his undergraduate studies in applied metaphysics at CalThaum, some, more recent additions acquired through his friendship with Jacob. He practiced the Art rarely these days, but he still maintained his license to practice, more to impress his clients than anything else. Tonight he had a feeling that he would need his skill, and as Jacob had admonished him, it didn't pay to ignore feelings when magic was involved.

Pietro met him at the door of the apartment looking haggard and frightened. He gave no greeting or explanation, just saying, "She's in here."

Egil followed him into Angelica's bedroom. At first he could see nothing wrong. Angelica was lying quietly in bed, looking peaceful and incredibly beautiful. He wanted to reach out and wake her, but a premonition stopped him. It was then that he noticed that except for the shallow breathing that moved the covers up and down she was motionless. There were none of the restlessness or small movements that mark normal sleep. Cautiously he lifted her eyelid. There was no response of the pupil to the light. The pulse in her wrist was steady but weak.

"How long has she been like this?"

"I don't know," Pietro said. "An hour, maybe two. We had supper together. She went to bed about eleven. I followed maybe half an hour later. She was fine when she went to bed. I had a dream, a nightmare. It woke me, and I came in here feeling something was wrong. She was like this then. She hasn't moved."

"Have you called a doctor?" Egil asked.

"No, she is not sick. She is bewitched. You know that as well as I do"

"Yes," Egil said. "Magnossi?"

"Si."

"And you are benandanti?"

"Yes, benandanti," Pietro said sadly.

"I think you had better tell me about it," Egil said.

"There is not much to tell, not really. It started when I was sixteen. I had a dream. A man came to me in my sleep. He said that he was the captain and that I was to follow him. I rose to do so, but when I turned back to look I saw my body still lying in the bed unmoving. I thought that I was dead, but the captain said that it would be all right. I would return to it before morning."

"We went on a journey. It didn't take long, but I knew that we had gone to a distant place. There was a field where we met the strega. We fought. That time we won. The captain took me home. When I woke in the morning I thought that it was just a crazy dream. I didn't know about the benandanti then. Our family was not one for superstition."

"That was in the spring. Nothing happened and I forgot it. Then in the fall I had the dream again where I followed the captain. When I woke, I had a big bruise on my side that I couldn't remember getting, but I still thought it was a dream. I went to the university soon after that, and I had no more dreams for two years, but then they came again. This time I did some research and learned what I was, what I had become. I was afraid. I did not want to be a witch. That was one of the reasons that I came to America. I thought that here I might escape from the captain."

"For a while I did. No dreams, no nocturnal journeys. I studied, received my doctorate, became a professor. Then, last year, I had another visit while I was asleep. It was from the captain. He told me of a man, Magnossi, who was a strega here in America. How he was a very bad man and I had to fight him. I didn't want to, but the captain made me. We went and did battle as we had done before, myself and some other benandanti, but now it was with Magnossi and his men, and not just in the spring and fall as it had been in Italy. We went out almost every month. Magnossi grew angry because we beat him sometimes, and even when we didn't he was too busy fighting us to engage in harm as he had done before."

"We knew what he was doing, about the protection racket he was running. That is why we fought him. We were cutting into his business, and that is why he tried to frame me. Now he has done this," Pietro said pointing at Angelica.

"Why didn't you tell me this before? It would have made my job a lot easier," Egil said.

"You weren't raised where I was. Italy is still a very superstitious place. Benandanti and strega are all one to most people. I was afraid, not for myself, but for Angelica. I didn't want the stigma attaching itself to her."

"I never wanted to be benandanti. I am a man of science, not magic. Since I first found out I have been asking myself if I was any better than the witches that we fought. I think I have been afraid of the answer. Sometimes, when we beat the witches off it felt good. Too good. Almost seductive. I was afraid that if I yield fully, if I admitted that I was benandanti, that I would be lost to it. I did not want that. Can you understand?"

"Yes," Egil said, "but if I had known, we might have made preparations. Set up some protections."

"Protections?"

"You don't know much about the Art, do you? Too narrow a specialization like most scientists."

"Can you do something about Angelica? I know that you care for her. That is why I called you."

"I'm not sure. I'm not familiar with this kind of magic. I'm not even a practicing wizard, really. I don't think that I had better attempt to counter the spell that might be dangerous. I've got a friend who is better at that than I am. But right now your sister is in a vulnerable condition. She has to be protected. Are you willing to help me?"

"Anything. I could not forgive myself if anything happened to Angelica."

"Good. First we have to move the bed so that the head points north." Egil removed a compass from his bag and checked the direction. He checked a book of tables to correct for the magnetic deviation. With Pietro's help he lifted the bed and put it in the proper orientation in the middle of the room. They cleared the rest of the furniture out so that he had more room to work in.

At each of the compass points he set up a tall white candle of beeswax in a silver holder and lit them so that they formed a diamond circumscribing the bed. Connecting the candles he drew lines with a piece of chalk closing each with a complicated flourish and an inscription in runes. At the institute his professors had always ragged him about using the ancient Norse symbols instead of the more conventional Hebrew and Greek, but he had insisted on doing so because of his Scandinavian heritage. Later, Jacob had said that he had been right. Control of magical forces draws on the soul, and his roots were in the north, not the Middle East.

Around the diamond he drew a pentagram with nine points, placing at each point the Norse word for the seven visible planets, the sun and the moon, reciting a chant in that language as worked. As he closed the last line of the pentagram the candle flames lengthened and bent in towards the middle to form an arch of fire covering the bed. Marachino's eyes widened and he crossed himself instinctively.

"I thought I was the witch," Pietro said quietly.

"Nothing, really," Egil said breathing heavily. The work had been painstaking and he was out of practice. "It's really just a question of channeling natural forces into certain patterns. A lot like an electromagnet. I've created a protective space around Angelica and no magical force should be able to get through to harm her body."

"Why hasn't she awakened, then?" Marachino asked.

"I thought you understood. I've protected her body, but the other part of Angelica, her mind or soul, or whatever you want to call it, isn't here. Magnossi has taken it with him."

☆　☆　☆　☆　☆

It was dawn when Egil finished the pentagram. He was tired and hungry from his work. The energy necessary to control the protective force had taken a lot out of him. To restore himself he went into the kitchen and began fixing some scrambled eggs.

"How can you stand there making breakfast? Angelica is in danger. We have to go to Magnossi and get her back."

"Look, Pietro, I've been up half the night. I'm in no shape to do much of anything right now, least of all to go rushing off to face Magnossi and a bunch of his goons. Besides, it wouldn't do any good. Angelica, at least the part of her that's missing isn't in this world. You of all people, being benandanti, should know that. My guess is that

Magnossi has her stashed on another plane of existence or where ever it is you wage your battles. I'm about at the limits of my magical knowledge, and even if I knew how to get to that place, I think we've got to be a lot stronger before we make an assault on it. One thing is for sure, Magnossi is going to be waiting for us and waiting in strength. Now eat some of these eggs. We're both going to need our strength."

Jacob didn't have a phone, saying that he didn't like them and didn't need one. Egil drove over after breakfast to fetch his mentor. The old man groused at coming, but packed a few things in an old carpet bag anyway.

When they arrived at the apartment Jacob went straight to Angelica's bedroom. Cautiously he walked around the perimeter of Egil's defenses, his nose sniffing the air like a bloodhound. Jacob always put a lot of faith in smelling magic, claiming that it was the most primitive and therefore the most sensitive of the senses.

"Ja, you are right, Egil. This Magnossi has taken away her soul. We must after it go."

"I'm ready," Marachino said eagerly.

"But I am not. This man is powerful. More powerful than you. More powerful than this Viking lawyer of yours. Maybe even more powerful than me. No, not that I think, but he will have help on his side. He does not fight alone. He will have his helpers with him. And one other, I think. Do you know who I mean?" Jacob asked pointedly.

"The Dark One?" Marachino asked.

"No, not Satan, but one of his demons at least, and not just any old demon, either. One of the Fallen."

"Then she is lost?"

"I didn't say that. The place of battle is not the Dark World. The demon will be bound by the rules of that place as much as we will. But we cannot go there lightly."

"We? What exactly do you have in mind, Jacob," Egil asked suspiciously.

"We must go and return with the girl's soul. Simple, no? You for courage, her brother for love, and me for brains. Or do I have that mixed up? One other we need, I think. Strength. This struggle in the place of battle is as much physical as magical. Do you still see that beefy Irish cop, Egil?"

"Yeah. I saw him a few days ago. He was the one that tipped me onto Magnossi's racket. You want Joe with us?"

"He's strong. Honest, too, if not too bright. From what you said he would like the goods on Magnossi get. No?"

"Yeah, but Joe isn't too comfortable with magic. He didn't fare too well the last time we got him involved in something."

"Then you must persuade him. Four we must have if we are to have a chance," Jacob said firmly.

"All right. I'll give him a call. But I can't guarantee anything."

"You will persuade him. We will go this night, then."

"Can't we go sooner?" Marachino pleaded.

"No. This is an affair of the night. It has always been so between the benandanti and the strega. The rules are set. We must conform to them. It is the only way."

It had taken some persuading to get O'Neil to come, particularly as he had pulled the evening shift. The three of them had waited anxiously for the policeman to show up, but the cop had finally knocked on the door just before midnight."

"This had better be good, counselor. You know I don't like any of this magic stuff, and I also don't like missing my sleep. As it is the missus will be thinking that I'm shacking up with some other broad," O'Neil said as he walked in.

"This is important, Joe. A girl's life is a stake. This also might be a good chance to get at Magnossi," Egil reassured him.

"Well let's get at it, then."

"Exactly," Jacob said. "We have only until dawn to complete our work. No more."

He led them into the bedroom. When O'Neil saw Angelica his eyes widened.

"Jesus. Is she dead?"

"No, but Magnossi has kidnapped her soul. We have to go after it," Egil explained.

"Saint's preserve us," O'Neil replied.

"We can hope," Jacob chimed in.

"Now we must each take up a position. There are four of us, four wards that Egil has set up. One of us should stand just outside the pentagram by each of the wards. Egil, you take the North because of your Viking ancestry. Pietro, the South for the same reason. That leaves East and West. That's obvious," Jacob said as he took up a position opposite the eastern ward.

"Is this a necessary part of the ritual?" Egil asked.

"No, but it can't hurt. The symbolism will tie us in to the world and give us more power. And believe me; we can use all we can get."

"The next part is relatively simple. I am going to put the four of us into a trance to simulate sleep. Pietro, you will have to be our leader, our captain, as you are the one who knows the way. As soon as you are under call each of us to follow you. Do you understand?"

"Yes, I understand," Marachino said grimly.

"Is that it?" Egil asked. "No preparations? No weapons? What are we supposed to fight with?"

"Remember, this is a journey in spirit. We will not be traveling corporally. Any weapons we had would not go with us. However, weapons of the spirit will accompany us if their hold on our imaginations is strong enough. Now we have wasted enough time."

The old man brought out an old fashioned gold watch suspended from a heavy gold chain. It glittered in the flickering light of the wards as it swung. Only moments passed before he had his three companions in a trance, then he stared hard at the watch and joined them.

Egil remembered watching the timepiece swinging in the light. He felt himself taking a step forward, moving into the flicker of the watch, yet drawing no nearer to it. Something compelled him to turn and when he did so, he saw his own body standing rigid and unmoving. It was an eerie experience yet he felt no fear, nor did he have any unusual sensations from the separation of his spirit and his corporal self.

The next thing he knew he was standing in the middle of a dirt road. The sun was shining, and they seemed to be in a valley flanked with fields on one side and woods on the other. In every direction he could see mountains in the distance, but he could not recognize their shape nor guess his location.

O'Neil was beside him, only he was dressed in his police blues, not in civilian clothes as he had been in the apartment. Dangling from the thong around his wrist was the polished black length of his night stick. His eyes darted around nervously as he took in his surroundings.

Marachino was there, too, on his other side. Like the policeman he had had a change of clothes and now was attired in a manner suitable to hiking through the Alps. Clutched in his right hand was a stalk of fennel some four feet long. From his reading, Egil recalled that this was a traditional weapon of the benandanti in their battles against witches.

He himself was dressed in an old pair of jeans and a flannel shirt, both of which he knew were lying in a drawer at his home, as were the boots on his feet. He also wore the old leather jacket that he used when camping. He found that he was carrying an ax, one that was identical to the one he had used to cut up firewood at his parents cottage when he was a kid. Its weight was comfortingly familiar, though he had not held it in a dozen years or more.

They had a moment to wait before Jacob appeared. The wizard was dressed in an old fashioned black coat and baggy trousers. His shirt had a high, stiff collar. On his head he wore a narrow brimmed hat of a style that had been common in Europe during the last century. To Egil, who knew the ways of his mentor, Jacob had assumed totally the identity of a nineteenth century rabbi from central Europe. Unlike the other three, he was weaponless, but Egil had expected nothing else. Jacob's weapons were not physical.

"Pietro, you know the way. Lead us," the old man said.

Marachino nodded and started down the road at a brisk pace. As they walked Egil took in their surroundings. The fields to their left small with narrow furrows. The wheat had already been harvested, the shocks standing to dry in the fields like a soldiers on guard. Nowhere was there any sign of machinery or other modern devices. This was farming as it had been before the introduction of mechanization.

They walked for half an hour or so, though they seemed to cover in that time a far greater distance than they should have. The sun was still high in the cloudless sky. Egil couldn't tell if it was moving or not. The air was cool, and not just from the lateness of the season. He had the impression that they were several thousand feet above sea level.

Pietro raised his hand and motioned them to a stop. "We are close now. The meeting place is just down this way." He pointed with his stalk to a narrow path that split off from the road they had been following. In the background they could hear the gurgling of a nearby creek.

They followed the path through the trees towards the creek. When they could see it they saw that on the far bank was a meadow a few hundred feet across that ran along the stream. In the center of meadow a rough hewn table had been set up flanked by benches. Four men sat on the benches or stood nearby. There was also a young woman with hair the color and length of Angelica's sitting next to one of the men.

A set of stepping stones provided a way across the creek. They crossed warily, instinctively fanning out and glancing from side to side looking for an ambush. Except for the four men at the table the meadow was deserted.

They slowly closed in on the table, their weapons at the ready. It was indeed Angelica at the table. Her hands and feet were bound and a gag had been tied over her mouth. The man next to her was Magnossi. He was dressed in a dark suit looking as coldly handsome as he had in the courtroom. The three men with him had stood now and seemed to have been cut from a mold. They were big, brutal men; hired muscle that looked as though they knew their business. One was armed with a hand sickle; the other two carried a baseball bat and a tire iron.

"So, you've come, Pietro," Magnossi said. "I told you that this was serious business and not to get in my way. I can hurt you; hurt you in more ways than one. I'm willing to make a deal, though. Leave. Go back to the old country and I'll give you back your sister. You can't win, you know."

"If I promise to go back to Italy you'll let her go?" Marachino asked cautiously.

"Yes. My word," Magnossi said, his voice smooth and calm. "Not right away, of course. Not until you are out of the country. But I'll let her go."

"No deal," Pietro said savagely.

"You benandanti, always stubborn. There's no other choice then. Boys."

The three thugs moved in on them. Their motions were practiced, as if they'd done this a hundred time before. O'Neil had his stick up and ready, his eyes locked onto those of the man with the tire iron. Egil was more uncertain. The ax was a familiar weight in his hand, but there was a big difference between chopping wood and going against a man. The sickle wielder sneered at him then suddenly struck out. The blade cut a glittering arc and he was just able to parry it at the last moment.

The ax proved an unwieldy weapon against the quickness of the lighter sickle. Egil fought desperately, backpedaling in the hopes of being able to use the reach advantage that the longer handle gave him. It was more luck than anything else that allowed him to catch the sickle with the head of the ax and send it spinning out of the grasp of his opponent.

There was fear in the other man's eyes, but Egil found that he couldn't use the ax. He wasn't a killer. He let the weapon drop and dove under the thug's right arm. Egil had never used his fists much, but he had wrestled in high school and college. It proved deceptively easy for him to duck around behind his man and get a shoulder lock on him. He squirmed around for a bit, but the lawyer was able to throw him to the ground. He kicked him twice when the thug tried to get up until finally he just lay there panting heavily.

The other battles had gone as quickly. The one O'Neil had faced was lying still on the ground with blood across his face and his ear raw and bleeding. The cop didn't look the worse for wear but he was breathing heavily. Marachino had also beaten his man, though his left eye was starting to puff up and the brow above it was cut. The man he had faced was in worse shape and was lying on the ground holding his gut.

"Impressive. You did better than I expected," Magnossi said, though he was still unruffled. "You chose your two friends wisely. But I was not depending on these. I have other, greater powers at my disposal."

There was a smell as of burning sulfur and Magnossi's face seemed to flow, the skin darkening and the jaw line elongating until it was a caricature of a human face. The ears became pointed and where the hairline had receded two small horns like those on a goat appeared. The eyes of the demon glowed brightly like the fires of the hell that had spawned it.

"Magnossi's soul is forfeit to me," the demon laughed, "and it is me that you face now. None of you will return from this place."

"No!"

It was Jacob who spoke, his voice filled with power that was not purely physical.

"Who are you to deny me?" the demon asked.

"I am just an old man, but yours is not the only power. I have lived long enough to have learned a thing or two."

'I am a prince of hell, old man. What is your power to me?"

"It is the light!" Jacob said and then he shouted a word. It made no sound in the ordinary sense, but the letters seemed to burn like fire in the air. They were in Hebrew, but Egil could make no sense of them. It was as if his mind wasn't strong enough to know them.

The demon knew their import, though. The word had frozen him in his tracks so that only his glowing eyes could move, and those eyes showed rage. The clothes on his body began to smoke and then burst into flames, separating to reveal skin that took on the color of heated iron just before it begins to glow red. The stench of burning sulfur was almost unendurable.

"Quick, Egil, untie the girl. We must leave this place quickly," Jacob ordered, his eyes fixed on the demon.

The lawyer did so, using a pocket knife he had found in his jeans to cut the ropes. Angelica was in his arms, her face buried in his chest to hide from the sight of the demon.

"All right. Back across the stream. Hurry." Jacob's voice was haggard, and there was sweat running down his forehead. Egil saw that the letters of the word had started to fade and that they no longer hung as high in the air.

They hurried towards the stream, O'Neil leading the way with Jacob bringing up the rear backing slowly away from the demon, his eyes always fixed on the word as if he were trying to keep it alive by sheer force of will. O'Neil reached the stream and splashed across. Marachino started to cross and Egil handed Angelica to him. Jacob was still fifty feet from the stream and the word was starting to fade rapidly. Egil started back for the old man. As he did so he saw one foot of the demon move.

"Egil, go back," Jacob shouted. "You can't save me. When the word extinguishes the demon will be free. I have no power left to hold him. Get across the stream and you'll be safe."

The word was now no more than a pale glow in air. The demon had taken a second step, moving in slow motion. Jacob had fallen to his knees still thirty feet from the stream.

"I can't leave you here," Egil cried as he reached toward him. The demon took two more steps, each faster than the one before. The word was scarcely visible. Grabbing Jacob's hand he pulled him up and threw him over his shoulder in a fireman's carry.

As he turned towards the stream he heard a roar from behind him. He knew that the word had vanished and that it was now a race between him and the demon to see if he could get to the stream before he was caught. Thirty feet had never seemed so far in his life. The old man was heavier than he looked. Behind him he could feel the presence of the demon closing in on him, he could hear the footsteps as they dug into the ground.

Suddenly his foot splashed into the stream. He could feel the water as it came up to his knee. The stream was narrow, only a few feet. A few more steps and he had reached the other bank. O'Neil was there pulling Jacob from his shoulder. Scrambling up the bank he threw himself on the ground. Marachino dragged him up and the two of them stumbled down the path after the policeman.

They made it to the road before stopping. O'Neil was panting heavily, but hadn't put down his burden. "What about that demon? Is it coming after us?"

"No. I think we're safe," Egil said. "It's the running water. Evil can't cross it. But I don't think we should linger here. Let's get going."

They took turns carrying the old man as they hurried down the road back the way had come. It took nearly an hour to make it back to their starting point, twice what it had taken on the way to the battle field. O'Neil, who had done the lion's share of the carrying, slumped to the ground. His form seemed to waver for a moment, then he was gone, followed quickly by Jacob. Angelica went next, then Marachino, leaving Egil to stare up the road for a few seconds before he took a step and returned to his proper world.

The four of them were again at their places by the wards, but this time they could see Angelica stirring on her bed. Her brother started forward but Egil called out, "Stop. Remember the wards. We can't get at her until I break the spell." Marachino nodded dumbly.

Angelica had come fully awake and looked about her, her eyes wide at the sight of wards. When she saw Egil she smiled and relaxed. The lawyer drew a silver dagger from his magic bag and, going to a particular spot on the pentagram, made three quick parallel cuts in the line. The sheet of light that had covered the bed split into its four component streams which drew back into the candles. Moving widdershins, Egil went to each candle in turn and snuffed out its flame. When the last one was out Angelica jumped out of the bed and into his arms.

"Egil, it was real, wasn't it? Not a dream?"

"No it was real, but you're safe now," he said stroking her hair gently.

"She may be safe, but I'm not," Jacob chimed up from his point on the east of the now disabled pentagram. "I've had a hard night's work for an old man and I need a drink before I die."

"I could use one too, counselor," O'Neil said. "I've seen too much this night to want to remain sober.

"Yes, I could use a drink as well," Marachino said as he led them from the room.

"And you, do need a drink?" Angelica asked.

"I have what I need," Egil replied before kissing her.

☆   ☆   ☆   ☆   ☆

Magnossi's body and the charred remains of his three henchmen were found in the burnt out ruins of a warehouse the gangster had owned. The charges against Pietro Marachino were officially dropped a few days later. Jacob recovered his strength after consuming half of a bottle of Chianti, most of the other half ending up inside of Joseph O'Neil. The policeman had some tall explaining to do both to his wife and his watch commander, but he was eventually forgiven by both of them after swearing never to get involved with anything magical again.

As for Angelica Marachino, a few months later she married a promising young lawyer of Norwegian descent.

HORRORSCOPE
BY GREG FOWLKES

A SHORT STORY FROM THE UPCOMING BOOK - *BACK ROAD TO THE STARS*

HORRORSCOPE

The apartment that the two men sat in was typical, or at least typical of what was expected for a bachelor in his early thirties making good money. It was comfortably furnished with an eye towards practicality rather than esthetics. Two bookcases dominated one wall but didn't quite suffice to bring order; magazines and books overflowed to stacks along the wall with a spread of the most recent on the coffee table between the two men. They were drinking beer. The bottles on the table carried a European label which they drank from tall pilsner glasses rather than from the bottles. Both men had reached a stage in life where comfort and style were of some importance.

All the trappings were there. Indeed, except for a slight lack of order, the apartment could have served as an example of the bachelor pad in Playboy. The leather and chrome, the three abstract prints on the wall, the stereo, all quite proper. The stereo consisted of a separate preamp and amplifier, Swiss turntable, a large Japanese tape deck with meters and knobs, and speakers, large speakers that stood in the corners. In this particular case the stereo was more than an idle toy. The owner knew more than a little about electronics. He also took his music serious as evidenced by the large and diverse record collection displayed in the rack next to the turntable.

The only jarring note, and that only slightly out of place, was a small electronics cabinet sitting on a table. Attached to it was what appeared to be a television set and a keyboard not quite like that of a typewriter. A few other more enigmatic pieces were connected to the cabinet to make a whole, that is a small computer of the type popular among hobbyists.

"Well, you've blown almost three thousand dollars on this gadget. What are you going to do with it?" Jim Wearing asked in a voice that indicated he thought his friend only slightly crazy.

"I don't know. I guess I'll find something to use it for. After all, I just got finished building it, give me time," the other answered somewhat defensively.

"Three grand is a lot of money to spend on something that you have to find a use for," Wearing said enjoying his friend's discomfort.

"What about that camera you bought last year. At the rate you've taken pictures with it, they're costing you about sixty dollars apiece."

"Okay, so I like expensive toys, too, but I still don't see what you need a computer for. It's not like you don't get your fill of them at work. You don't have to have one at home, too. Just give me one good use for it."

Ernie Skoog thought for a moment, not quite sure if he wanted to admit it, but he was being pressed hard by Wearing, and he wasn't about to yield. "For one thing, I'm thinking of using it to calculate astrological charts."

"Astrological charts," Wearing sputtered, not quite able to control himself. "You mean you bought this thing to cast horoscopes? You don't really believe in that stuff, do you?"

"No, not really," Skoog admitted unconvincingly. "But it is an interesting problem. The calculations, I mean. You have to keep track of the sun and the moon. All the planets, too. That means storing some sort of ephemeris in a way that the computer can access. It's not at all a simple matter, and it's a damn sight more interesting than some of the problems that I have to solve at work."

"But horoscopes, Ernie. How did you ever get involved with that sort of thing? What would they do at the plant if they found out one of their programmers was into mumbo jumbo?"

"I don't know. It's just a hobby. I started to learn about it in college. I met this girl who was into it. I wanted to impress her."

"A good enough motive. How did you do?" Wearing asked with a leer.

"She took up with a football player and left me with a dozen books on astrology. It seemed a waste not to read them, and once I did, I got interested. It was a good break from my studies. Something that I could relax with. Like I said, a hobby."

"Okay, okay. I guess I won't start worrying about your sanity until you show up at work with a ring in your ear and begin reading palms. So tell me oh mighty seer, how do you go about casting your charts and predicting the future?"

"Astrology doesn't predict the future, it just determines the influences. But as to the mechanics, I take the exact time and place of birth and determine the locations of the various planets at that time. Then for any future date I can calculate what factors will exert a positive or negative influence on that person. All the computer does is make the calculations simpler for me. It can do a couple of hours work in a few minutes."

"Show me," Wearing said, showing some interest.

"Okay," Skoog said, "I'll need the exact time and place of your birth." Wearing answered and Skoog entered the information with the keyboard. "Now, the computer is printing out the planets that were influences at your birth. You can see it prints what house of the zodiac they were in and their positions within the house, that is whether they were ascending or descending." The printer clattered away as it constructed a table of the information. "If we pick a date at random, say the end of this month, the computer will give the position of the planets on that date, and using that as a basis, the influences can be determined.

Ernie made the entry and after a moment the printer clattered to life again. Wearing read the printout.

"All very impressive, swami, but what does it mean. Will I meet a tall, dark stranger, or fall into a lot of money?"

"Horoscopes really only point up the influences," Ernie said as he studied the printout. "It doesn't look too good, actually. There are a lot of sinister influences coming into play. Maybe I should try another date."

"No, I think I've had all the bad news I want," Wearing said flippantly.

It was a week before the subject of horoscopes came up again. This time it was at work, and Ernie came into Wearing's office with a worried look and a stack of computer printouts.

"What's up? You look like you've got problems," Wearing said observing his friend's expression.

"Yeah. I've come across something that I don't understand, and it's got me scared silly."

"Well, out with it," Wearing said a little impatiently.

"You remember when I cast your chart. It came out pretty grim."

"If you believe in that kind of thing."

"Anyway, I was casting a chart for a friend for the same day. It came out just as bad. The influences were all negative. Well, as a check, I did a couple more for other people that I knew, all for the same day, the end of this month. They all turned out bad, without exception."

"Looks like it's going to be a bad day, then," Wearing said jokingly. "Maybe we should all just stay in bed."

Ernie didn't take the bait. More seriously, he commented, "Isn't it possible that there's a bug in your program? It wouldn't be the first time that sort of thing has happened. Remember when that evaluation program we had slipped a decimal point a couple of months ago?"

"Don't you think that I thought of that? All this week I've been running the program. There's nothing unusual except for the last day of this month. Just to make sure, I worked out a couple of charts by hand as a cross check. I got the same results. No matter how I do the calculations, the last day of this month is really rotten. For everyone, or at least everyone that I've done a chart on. I've even taken to picking birth dates at random and working out the charts. Same results without a single deviation."

Wearing had seen his friend worked up like this before, but only when he had been confronted with a problem that really stumped him. In such cases he would continue with dogged determination to reach a solution, practically excluding everything else from his life. He had no desire to have Ernie work up such an obsession now, not over astrology.

"Look, you said yourself that you don't really believe in this stuff. Why don't you just forget it?"

"Because I want to know why every chart I work out shows doom and destruction for the last day of this month, that's why. There must be a reason for it.

"It's just a coincidence, some odd positioning of the planets or something. Take my advice and drop it."

Ernie had left the office after that, and he didn't say anything more about the subject, but Wearing could tell that he didn't intend to drop the business. Other matters distracted him for the next couple of days, but as the end of the month rolled around, Ernie became more and more agitated, even withdrawn. It was clear that the thing was preying on his mind. His work was suffering, too, though not so much that it was causing a problem — at least one that couldn't be ignored for a couple of weeks. Wearing just wished that the end of the month would pass so that Ernie would forget about his dire predictions and return to normal.

The end of the month came and nothing dire happened, except, that is, for Ernie's not showing up for work. It didn't cause any hassles as the project he was on was still on schedule. He had plenty of sick days coming to him, too. In fact, he had never used any of what was coming to him since he had started working at the plant. Even when he had had the flu and a temperature of 101, he had come into work.

Wearing meant to call, but somehow the day passed and he didn't have the time. Still, he was a little worried, so he decided to drive over after dinner and see if his friend was all right.

The apartment was considerably messier than the last time Wearing had visited. Printouts were strewn everywhere and a big chart had been tacked up above the computer. Ernie himself looked a little haggard. There were a couple of empty beer bottles scattered about and the ashtray was almost overflowing. Wearing noted the latter because his friend had given up smoking six months earlier. Now he had one in his mouth and a butt was still smouldering in the ashtray.

"Did you think that you could get the day off just because it's the end of the world?" Wearing had asked when Ernie had opened the door. The joke had fallen flat.

"If you've come here to crack jokes, you can leave. I'm busy."

Wearing was taken aback. In the three years that he had known Ernie that was the first time he had ever seen him display anger at another person.

"Look, I'm sorry. You weren't at work today. I just came by to see if you were alright. You've been letting yourself get awfully worked up about this astrology thing."

"Yeah, well this 'astrology thing' has got me damned worried. In the past three weeks I've done about eight thousand charts for the last day of this month, today, and so far not one of them has been without overwhelmingly negative influences. Not one. That's not a coincidence, that's not even a trend, that's a certainty. There's nothing particularly special about the position of the planets, but still, every chart I work up for today comes out bad. I can't explain it, but when I see it written in front of me like that I start to wonder. Then I start to worry. What would you do?"

"I don't believe in this nonsense, and I can't believe that you do either. After all, you're not some half educated crazy, and this isn't the middle ages. You're a computer programmer and a damned good one. Science is what you believe in, not some half baked mumbo jumbo."

"Yeah, and all the science I've ever learned tells me that what I've been calculating can't happen. There's no room for a coincidence this big. It's like the quantum mechanical probability of an elephant tunneling through a brick wall. There has got to be some reason for all these charts coming out predicting death and destruction, and I want to know why."

"Look, I don't know why your charts keep coming out the way they do, but I do know what they're doing to you. You've been worse than useless at work, and now today you didn't show up at all. If you keep going on like this, you're going to get in trouble."

"I know, but I'm scared. I see something, and I don't understand it. I'm scared that I just might be right. Up until I cast your chart, the first one, this was all a game to me. I didn't believe in it. It was just a hobby, an outlet; like model railroading. But this. Statistics tells me that it can't happen. Common sense tells me it can't happen. But it happens, and I start to wonder if there's a cause behind the effect. Maybe this astrology stuff isn't garbage. After all, it dates back three, four thousand years, maybe more than that. Stonehenge is five thousand years old, and it's nothing more than an astrological computer. Maybe they knew something back then. If it were all rubbish, somebody would have noticed in all that time, wouldn't they."

"Listen to yourself, Ernie. You've gotten so worked up about this anomaly that you're actually believing in the whole thing. Maybe you have come across something strange, some quirk of positioning that makes every chart you calculate on that little computer of yours look grim as hell, but that's just a problem of mathematics with some kind of rational solution, not a reason to start believing in the powers of the planets and stars to influence peoples' lives. The two aren't in any way related. You should be able to see that."

Ernie sat down and wiped his face with his hand. He looked tired. Wearing doubted that he had had any sleep in the last couple of days. At least he didn't look like he had.

"I know I shouldn't believe in this, but I'm scared. I've worked it out for eight thousand people, real and theoretical, and it looks like they will all die sometime today. But that's not what has me scared. Those are other people."

He took a pull on a beer bottle that had been sitting untouched for over an hour, then continued, "You know after I worked up the first few charts and they all came out the same way, I was afraid to do my own; afraid that it would show bad things, too. Not very rational, I admit. At first I just didn't want to put in any bias to my thinking, but then I was afraid. I finally worked up the courage last night to do it. It looks just as grim as all the others. That's what has me scared."

"No one wants to know when he's going to die," Wearing said softly. "The point is, you aren't going to die. All of this," he swept his hand around the room to indicate the charts laying everywhere, "it's not real, Ernie. It's all a sham and pseudo science. We both know that. You've gotten excited, and now you're tired and just not thinking straight."

Ernie hesitated before replying. "Yeah, maybe you're right. I guess I am tired, and I've let things get out of hand." He seemed to slump down into his chair as if a weight had been lifted from him."

"Get some sleep. It'll all look better in the morning."

"If there is a morning," Ernie said, but this time there was a hint of humor in his voice despite his fatigue.

"It's almost eleven thirty now, and nothing has happened. I'm going home and getting some sleep myself. Why don't you sleep late tomorrow? I don't think they'll miss you if you skip another day of work."

"Yeah, sounds like a good idea." He got up and showed Wearing to the door.

Returning, he thought about going to bed, but despite the state of his body, he didn't feel relaxed enough to sleep. "What I need is a drink," he said to himself. He had gone down to the liquor store in the morning, intending to do some heavy drinking before the end. He had gotten the most expensive bottle of scotch he could find, but somehow he hadn't gotten around to opening it all day. Now was the time that he needed it, and there was no sense in wasting good booze. He poured himself a healthy glassful over ice and then went to the stereo. He picked his favorite recording, one of the Brandenburgs, and sat down, letting the music and the whiskey mellow him out.

They were doing the job of relaxing him when he heard a rumble in the distance. It subsided for a moment, and then increased. The lights flickered, and the needle jumped on the record. Outside he could hear screams and the wailing of a siren. The lights went out entirely, and he used a match to light a candle that had been sitting on the table next to him. Outside the wind was howling. He heard a crash, then another. The rumble was now great enough to be felt.

Strangely, he was no longer scared. He knew what was coming, what he had suspected. The charts hadn't been wrong. They couldn't be, not that many times. He sipped his whiskey slowly, regretting only that the stereo had stopped playing. It didn't really matter, though. It would all be over soon. The whole world would be over.

The Fictional Detective
By Greg Fowlkes

Now available from
The Fictional Press

Read the first chapter!

THE FICTIONAL DETECTIVE
CHAPTER ONE

I was sitting in my office staring at the frosted glass of the door. It was a cold and rainy Friday morning in October and I had a hangover that made my head feel as faded and peeled as the paint on the walls. The half empty glass of Jack Daniel's wasn't helping my head any, but it was making it easier to ignore some of my other problems. Like how I was going to pay three months back rent on the eight by ten closet the landlord chose to call an office. Jobs had been pretty scarce lately. Even the divorce business had fallen off. No one seemed to care what their spouse was up to anymore. Not for the first time I wondered what the world was coming to.

A sharp rapping sound came that I thought at first was my brain shattering. A second later I realized that it was the tap of knuckles on the glass of the door. The lights were off in the office, and it couldn't have looked very promising from the outside, but the knuckles kept up the rapping. Looking through the "evitceteD ,EDALS KNARF", printed backwards on the frosted glass I could see the form of the rapper silhouetted by the sixty watt bulb in the hallway. t was a woman, and a good looker by the shadow.

The rapping stopped and the shadow moved away. I cursed myself for being too slow, but then she returned and rapped once more. The knuckles had a sort of desperate sound to them so I told her to come in, trying to keep my voice from sounding too harsh. The door opened hesitantly and she stepped through into the darkened office. She stood in the doorway groping for the light switch.

The bank of overhead fluorescents came on with a stutter and the light made me wince. I didn't mind so much when I got a good look at the dame. Her shadow hadn't done her justice at all. She was tall, looking taller on her spiked heels. Her eyes, a soft green gray would have almost been level with my own if I had been standing. Remembering my manners a moment later, I was. She smiled at my courtesy and her warm, red lips almost made my legs melt beneath me. Blonde hair curled under just at her shoulder line. I got a good look at it up close when I stepped forward to help her out of her coat; it looked natural. Everything about her looked natural though she was too good to believe.

I don't normally go overboard treating women with respect. These days it doesn't really pay, but this broad had class. Under her coat she was dressed in a black dress that clung to her like a sheath from her neck to her nylon clad calves, but despite the sensuous curves she looked like she was in mourning.

I held out a chair for her and then took one myself. Self-consciously I put the cap back on the bottle of whiskey and put it and the glass away in a drawer. "What can I do for you, Miss . . . ?" I couldn't see if she had a wedding ring on underneath her gloves, but I had the distinct impression that she wasn't married.

"Janet, Janet Nielsen," she said in a soft voice that reminded me of the taste of good bourbon — smooth and mellow but with a bite to it. "You are Mr. Frank Slade, are you not?"

"That's what it says on the door," I answered. She hadn't made a mistake. I had no illusions about my reputation and Miss Nielsen looked like she had the money and the class to get the best in town.

"I wish to employ your services if you are available, Mr. Slade. It's a matter of some importance to me and I am quite willing to pay you well if you can start immediately."

"I think I can shift my schedule, Miss Nielsen," I said, aware that I had no schedule or clients either. "What is it you want me to do? You didn't correct me when I said 'Miss', so I'm guessing you don't want me to check up on an errant husband. Or do you?"

"No, nothing like that," she said with a note of distaste. "A friend of mine died recently under mysterious circumstances. The police are saying that it was either an accident or suicide. I have reason to believe it was murder."

"Look, Miss Nielsen," I said, "I'd like to help you out, but if its murder, it's a business for the cops and I can't get involved. I could lose my license."

"But if the police say that it's not murder, then you are free to investigate. That's right, isn't it?" she said, assuredly. I wasn't used to getting that much logic out of a woman. "I will pay you two hundred dollars a day plus expenses. That will be adequate, I believe. I have a thousand dollars here as an advance against the first five days."

She opened her purse and pulled out ten crisp, new hundred dollar bills and laid them out on the blotter of my desk. I needed that money, but I was getting a little suspicious of the whole thing. It was too much like the opening of a detective novel; a beautiful woman, a hard boiled private investigator, a stack of brand new large denomination bills.

"Look, I'm still not sure I can do anything for you. Why don't I take a day's pay and check things out with the cops? If I think I can do anything for you, I'll come back and get the rest of the money. If not, we can call it even." I looked into those gray green eyes. She hesitated for a moment, and then nodded. I slid two bills from the pile, and then slid the rest back towards her. She didn't pick them up.

"Okay. Now why don't you tell me who this friend of yours was, and how he died?" I was watching her closely for her reaction as I asked.

"Do you know of Ezekial O. Handler?"

"The mystery writer?" I asked.

"Yes," she answered. For the first time she seemed to lose some of her composure. I wondered why. Handler was pretty well known as a writer. He had written a dozen or more books, a couple of which had made the best seller lists. I'd met him once or twice in the course of my work, but we definitely did not move in the same circles.

"Last night his car went off the road along West Shore Drive. They said it was traveling at a high rate of speed and crashed through the barrier. The car burned and Ezekial burned with it."

"That sounds like an ordinary traffic accident to me, Miss Nielsen," I said, trying not to sound callous.

"But it couldn't have been. He was a very good driver. He never took chances, either. Not stupid ones, at least. He wasn't the kind of man who felt that he had to prove anything, least of all to himself. No, if his car crashed there was a reason for it."

"If there was, I'm sure the police will find it," I said. I didn't like what I had to say next, she obviously had some sort of emotional tie to Handler, but in my business there are a lot of things you have to do that you don't like. "That is if it was an accident. It might have been a suicide. I didn't know Handler personally, but writers aren't always the most stable sort of people. It goes with the artistic temperament. Could he have had any reason for killing himself?"

"No, of course not," she said very defensively. "He had everything to live for. He was well off financially, he had a lot of good friends, he'd just finished his last book and it was one of his best. He stood to make a good deal of money from it, at least a million dollars. He was a happy man, Mr. Slade. I know that he was."

"Just what was your relationship to Handler, Miss Nielsen? Why are you so interested in proving that he was murdered?"

I thought she might clam up then or get huffy, but she said right out loud, "I was his mistress." Just like that, not like she was ashamed of it or anything. Maybe she wasn't. These days who could tell? "I loved him, Mr. Slade, and if he was murdered I want the murderer brought to justice."

I raised my eyebrows at that. Handler had pushed past fifty as far as I knew and he wasn't much of a looker, either. The pictures on his book jackets showed a nose that had been broken in fights a couple of times. When I'd seen him he'd proved to be a short man, though powerfully built. He had a reputation for getting into fights. He didn't seem the sort that would appeal to the woman across the desk from me, but like I always said, who can tell these days.

"I know what you're thinking, that he was thirty years older than me, but I never cared about that. He was always very good to me, kind and gentle. I admit to being a kept woman, Mr. Slade, but that doesn't mean that I didn't love him."

There was something strange about that phrase - kept woman - that seemed out of place. It was more like something from one of Handler's books than what a young, liberated woman should be saying. I didn't doubt that it was true, though. It would explain where Nielsen's money came from. Listening to her, I could believe that she had loved him, too.   Either that or she was a mighty good actress.

"I'll take your word for it that he was wealthy and happy, but there are other reasons a man kills himself. What about his past? Could there be some secret there? Or his health? Hemingway killed himself because of cancer, after all."   Handler wasn't quite in the same league, but I hoped the comparison might mollify her a little.   The last couple of questions hadn't improved her opinion of me.

"I don't know too much about his past. He never talked much about it. He always seemed to live in the present. He's been a public figure for twenty-five years, though. I don't think he could have had many secrets. He never seemed to care what people thought about him anyway, as long as they read his books."

"Maybe he cared about what you thought?" I said.

She smiled at that and I thought I was going to melt again. "No, I don't think so. He was fond of me, but the love was all one way. The only opinions that really matters to him were his own. He never seemed to mind the critics."

"What about his health, then?   He was getting on in years."

"I can assure you; he kept in very good shape.   He always ran four or five miles before he'd start writing in the morning. He was in good shape other ways, too," she said in a wistful tone that made me wish I'd been the late Mr. Handler. "He'd just been to a doctor a couple of weeks ago for an insurance examination. They must not have found any problems because he got the policy." I could believe her on that.   Handler had been something of a physical fitness nut.   I could remember the deep chest and the boxer's shoulders.

"Well, we'll rule out suicide for the moment," I said. "But he still might have had an accident. Some drunken fool might have run him off the road. It could have happened. If so, I'm afraid you'll just have to face it. But I'll check with the cops and go out and look at the scene of the crash myself. If I see anything suspicious I'll check up on it, Miss Nielsen. '

"Thank you, I'm sure you will. Will that be all, now?"

"Yes, I think so. If I have any more questions I'll get in touch with you." She gave me her address and phone number, then rose to leave.

"Miss Nielsen?"

"Yes?"

"You forgot your eight hundred dollars," I said, though part of me was cursing myself for being a fool.

"Thank you, Mr. Slade," she said, picking up the bills and dropping them into her purse. I helped her on with her coat, smelling again the warm, sweet scent of her hair. Then she was gone.

THE FICTIONAL DETECTIVE IS NOW AVAILABLE FROM THE FICTIONAL PRESS. FIND OUT MORE AT WWW.FICTIONALPRESS.COM

Now From Resurrected Press

SCIENCE FICTION AUTHORS RESURRECTED

Fyfe Resurrected - The Works of H. B. Fyfe
Stories from the Golden Age of Science Fiction by the author of D-99. dealing with the interaction of humans and aliens on far off worlds in ways that were as creative as they were imaginative.

Bone Resurrected - The Stories of J. F. Bone
More stories from the Golden Age of Science Fiction. Includes "The Issahar Artifact," "Assassin," "To Choke an Ocean" and more.

Nourse Resurrected - The Stories of Alan E. Nourse
Stories from the Golden Age of Science Fiction. Includes "Contamination Crew." "Coffin Cure," "The Link," and more.

Dick Resurrected - The Early Stories of Philip K. Dick
Early stories from the author of the novels that inspired "Blade Runner," "Total Recall," and "A Scanner Darkly".

Other Classic Science Fiction Novels
Being Resurrected Soon

Talents, Incorporated - By Murray Leinster
When a Mekinese fleet conquers his home planet, Captain Bors turns to Talents, Incorporated for help using their collection of individuals with unusual abilities to defeat the enemy and save the galaxy.

The Pirates of Ersatz - by Murray Leinster
Bran Hodden just wanted to be an electronic engineer and marry a delightful girl. But when he's framed by the powers on Walden he's forced to turn back to his family's trade, piracy. Also published as The Pirates of Zan.

Empire - by Clifford Simak
Spencer Chambers and Interplanetary Power owned the Solar System because they controlled the source of power. It fell to Russell Page and Harry Wilson to challenge that control if they had to cross the universe to do it.

Night of the Long Knives - The Creature from the Cleveland Depths - by Fritz Leiber
Two classic novellas set in the not too distant future from a classic master of science fiction.

Armageddon - 2419 A.D. - The Air Lords of Han - by Phillip Francis Nowlan
The two novels that introduced the world to that intrepid hero of the 25th Century, Buck Rogers. Buck Rogers must save the world from the clutches of the insidious Han.

Other Classic Resurrected Science Fiction Edited by Greg Fowlkes

Resurrected Martians
Classic Stories about Mars and Martians from the Golden Age of Science Fiction

Resurrected Aliens
Classic Stories of Aliens and Alien Encounters from the Golden Age of Science Fiction

Resurrected Flying Saucers
Classic Stories of Flying Saucers and Alien Invasions from the Golden Age of Science Fiction

Resurrected Robots
Classic Stories of Robots, Cyborgs and Androids from the Golden Age of Science Fiction

Resurrected Space Ships
Classic Stories of Space Ships from the Golden Age of Science Fiction

Resurrected Time Travel
Classic Stories of Time Travel from the Golden Age of Science Fiction

Resurrected Dimensions
Classic Stories of other Dimensions from the Golden Age of Science Fiction

Resurrected Futures
Classic Stories of the Far Future from the Golden Age of Science Fiction

Resurrected Mad Scientists
Classic Stories of Mad Scientists and their Creations from the Golden Age of Science Fiction

Resurrected Monsters
Classic Stories of Monsters and Mayhem from the Golden Age of Science Fiction

THE FICTIONAL DETECTIVE
BY GREG FOWLKES

Who killed Ezekial O. Handler?

A beautiful dame, a hard-boiled private eye — and a dead body.

It started like any other case. When a famous writer dies in a mysterious car crash, private detective Frank Slade is called in to find answers, but all he finds is more questions. Who killed Ezekial Handler? Who is Janet Nielsen and why is she so interested in finding out? Who is leaving the neatly typed clues?   And as Slade tries to find answers to these questions he starts to wonder if the ultimate answer will threaten his very existence.

Read about it in
THE FICTIONAL DETECTIVE
Visit www.thefictionaldetective.com

The Fictional Press
www.TheFictionalPress.com

The Fictional Press is an imprint of Intrepid Ink, LLC. Find out more at www.TheFictionalPress.com.

About Intrepid Ink, LLC

Intrepid Ink, LLC provides full publishing services to authors of fiction and non-fiction books, eBooks and websites. From editing to formatting, from publishing to marketing, Intrepid Ink gets your creative works into the hands of the people who want to read them. Find out more at www.IntrepidInk.com.